"We are leaving immediately," P002 repeated. "I will identify the target and direct the attack."

707 turned and gave 777 a meaningful stare before walking out with 701. When 777 turned back, P002 was staring at him again. The pair had had multiple disagreements during the planning and training phase of the mission on the flight out to Pyriat-2. In his own unit, disagreements and discussions about plan effectiveness were normal. They were even encouraged by their leader, 707. He wanted their plans picked apart and stress-tested before the first foot hit the ground to make sure his battlesynths weren't put in unnecessary risk nor were any innocent lives.

P002 was different. He was driven to prove he was not an inferior model. Among their kind, the word *prototype* was practically a slur, and one that the synth reacted strongly to. The resentment and contempt he felt toward battlesynths was something he wasn't able to fully hide. 777 was concerned the emotional instability of their commander would compromise the mission. What he would also like to know was why the original mission commander, 707, had been replaced by a synth that had never actually been assigned to an active military unit.

"There is little we can do at this point," 707 said. "We will address this with Ministry Command after the mission. For now, follow orders."

"Understood," 777 said.

The assault on the rebel leader's position had gone as expected. Their defenses had been surprisingly well-organized, but the results were inevitable. The battlesynths hit them hard and fast, breaking through their northern emplacement and quickly getting in behind the other defender strongholds and crushing them completely. When 777 began the assault on the final position by the river, however, he saw that the area was not clear of innocent civilians as they'd been briefed. Not even close.

Large groupings of screaming civilians, including children, were trying to huddle behind what little cover there was as three groups of battlesynths rushed through the streets. 777 and 701 both fired their repulsors, arcing up and over the few individual skirmishes. 777 slammed down right in the middle of a barricaded position and went to work. The stunned soldiers didn't get a single shot off before his arm cannons reduced everything and everyone behind the hasty barrier to slag. 701 had come down just behind the position and waited for him before heading up the steps to the armored door their target was supposed to be behind.

"Hold!" P002 called, running fast up the street toward them. "Hold there!"

"We are moments from the objective," 777 objected when P002 got to them. "Every second of delay risks his escape."

"I will handle the capture," P002 said. "It is imperative that no mistakes are made. Now, you will—" his speech was cut short by the doors opening of their own volition. A young, tall Pyriasian male walked out with his hands out from his sides.

"Please...no more violence is needed," he said. "I am willingly your prisoner, just do not hurt any more of my people."

"You are in no position to make demands," P002 said, shoving the unarmed Pyriasian into 701's arms. "You are nothing but a terrorist with delusions of grandeur."

"You come here because your superiors tell you to." The young rebel shook his head sadly. "You slaughter us in droves because you're powerful, and it's easy for you, but did you ever stop and think *why* you're killing us? I know of your kind. Do you ever think about all the thousands each of you must have killed in your long lives?"

"Who are *you* to lecture *me*?" P002 said with such vehemence that 777 stepped back and turned toward him. "Our orders were to capture you, but they said nothing of the rest of your rabble."

"What are you doing?" 777 demanded.

"Xeta Detachment, eliminate all biotics within the perimeter," P002 said over the com.

"No!" the Pyriasian screamed, struggling in vain against 701's grip.

"What are you doing?!" 777 repeated.

"I don't answer to you," P002 whirled on him. "One more word, and I will include your insubordination on my report, and you can enjoy a fresh round of behavior conditioning."

777 watched as the other battlesynths opened fire on the screaming civilians. They waded in and slaughtered entire family groups with no mercy. He looked and saw 707 standing by himself, not participating. His glowing red eyes were focused wholly on P002, who was too engrossed in the killing to notice or care.

"Watch until the end," P002 said, kneeling to his captor's level. "Their deaths are on your head. Remember that."

Xeta Detachment was retrieved and taken off-world quickly as the use of battlesynths against non-military targets was a politically sticky subject. P002 had handed the prisoner over without incident, and their superiors seemed disinterested to learn that the mission commander had ordered the pointless butchering of a couple hundred innocent civilians. They were more excited at how quickly the battlesynths had secured their objective.

Combat Unit 777 stared out into space as the ConFed transport flew them away from Pyriat-2. He could feel it. Something had changed in him down there. If he had to put a word to it, he would call it disillusionment. His maker had told him that he was built for a glorious, noble purpose, but all he could feel at the moment was shame and remorse.

"It will not always be like this," 707 said from behind him.

"Yes, it will," 777 said. "They now know they can use us against others and, as long as the outcome is politically acceptable, so will be the collateral damage."

"Perhaps. I have already reported the incident to Ministry Command. They have agreed to a hearing. P002 will likely be decommissioned for this atrocity."

"How does that change things for the better? I could have stopped him. I was standing right there."

"And the battlesynths near would have seen you attack your superior, turning their guns on you. Is that a better outcome?"

"Perhaps it would have been."

707 left him to his ruminations. Battlesynths were not slaves, but nor were they exactly free to just roam as they pleased. There were some bureaucratic hurdles to get over, but 777 felt his destiny had just partially revealed itself. He would not be used as a weapon against innocent beings. It was time for him to leave and strike out on his own. He hoped the other members of Lot 700 would understand that.

1

"How...long?"

"You have been unconscious for over six days," Lucky said to Kage, helping him into a seated position. "You were badly injured. I sought help, now we are captured."

"Got it," Kage said, closing his eyes again. "Captured by whom?"

"A Vissalo," Lucky said. "His name in Ancula."

"Doesn't sound promising," Kage said. "Didn't we piss off a Vissalo once before?"

"Bondrass."

"That's right. He was an asshole."

"This one does not appear to be any better."

"The others get away?"

"I assume so," Lucky said. "At least I hope the captain's judgment was such that he left with the others."

Kage said nothing else. He knew that Lucky's new body contained a miniaturized slip-com burst transmitter and probably assumed the battlesynth had sent a message to the captain telling him to leave without them. He was also smart enough to not say any of this aloud in a room undoubtedly being monitored by their captors.

Omega Force had been operating on a massive logistics platform called The Gates. It was the commerce hub for a frontier expanse called the Luuxir Border Region, and also the choke point for multiple trafficking rings that had been preying on the refugee convoys and colony ships. They'd originally come there to take out a specific target that Lucky had been familiar with when he'd been trapped in his own mind as *Seven*. However, they'd stumbled onto something far larger and more dangerous than they had bargained for.

In the course of trying to take down the source of the trafficking operation and coordinate with outside parties to rescue the abductees, Kage had been grievously wounded. Lucky had been forced to find an unconventional solution to help his friend since Doc had been unavailable and the *Phoenix*—along with her infirmary—had been sitting powerless in a cave with her right wing blown off. His efforts had led him aboard a starship owned by a Vissalo, who agreed to help Kage in exchange for Lucky's service, but the exact terms had been nebulous and, so far, they'd been left alone while the Veran recovered. Lucky feared that meant that Ancula had plans for them both.

What had been the biggest shock for Lucky was a figure from his past being aboard the ship. A prototype battlesynth unit called P002 had been there to greet him, now calling himself Suta, a Vissalian word meaning *most favored blade*. From what Lucky could surmise, Suta was Ancula's personal enforcer. What he couldn't figure out was why the synth was alive at all. After slaughtering hundreds of innocent civilians, the Ministry of Martial Affairs had assured them that P002 had been decommissioned and dismantled, yet here he was.

Suta still looked the same as he had. He was built using a standard synth chassis, so he was shorter than Lucky. To that, the pru engineers had added armor, arm cannons that couldn't be retracted, upgraded actuators to handle the additional weight, and a hotter powerplant. He was one of the progenitors of what would become

Now that he knew Ancula wanted Seven and his mimic capability —both of which were gone—he was no longer sure he and Kage wouldn't just be disposed of for convenience. He was confident he could fight his way off the ship and survive, but it would mean leaving Kage to die, and that was something he wouldn't consider even for a moment. He needed a way to make himself indispensable again to whatever plan Ancula had.

"It appears you were being honest," Suta said once the scan was complete. "How unfortunate for you."

2

"He is coming your way."

Jason timed it almost perfectly, and he stepped out between the buildings just in time to clothesline the sprinting *intara*, sending him flipping into the air before slamming face down into the hardpacked dirt of the alley.

"Oh, shit! I know that hurt. Where were you going in such a hurry, Orthin?"

"Away from you, you crazy bastard," Orthin wheezed out, trying to catch his breath. "I saw what you did to the last guy who wouldn't talk."

"So, wouldn't it make more sense to just talk?" Jason asked, squatting in front of the alien as 701 came running up, covering the way the alien had just come from.

"You'd think so, but no," Orthin said. "If the local guild finds out I'm cooperating with you, I'll lose my franchise."

"If you don't cooperate with me, you'll lose something more valuable. Like your legs."

"When did you become so sadistic, Burke? Didn't you used to have a code?

"Times change, I change with them," Jason said piously. "Now... what's it going to be? Talky-talky or choppy-choppy." He pulled out and activated a wicked, curved molecular vibro-blade that Crusher had gifted to him. The ultrasonic whine was an unpleasant accompaniment to Orthin's whimpering.

"Please, damn you!" he whispered desperately. "You can't do this in the open. Just get me someplace secure and don't chop anything off that won't grow back."

At that, Jason looked quizzically at 701 who, in turn, gestured to his groin area. Jason nodded his understanding.

"That will depend entirely on you. Hand me whatever credits you're carrying," Jason said softly, still waving the blade around. "Quickly."

"You're *robbing* me?"

"You want to put on a show that's believable or not? Hand it over. Now."

"I'd almost rather you chopped a leg off," Orthin grumbled, taking out a handful of chits totaling well over twenty-thousand credits.

"Where the fuck were you going with all this?"

"There's a place down the way that has these girls from—"

"Never mind," Jason said. "You know where my ship is parked. Meet me there, and I'll give you your cash back. Bring a gun and look angry when you come up the ramp."

"You're serious?"

"I'm trying to be a team player here, Orthin, but if you insist on being this stupid, I'm just going to shoot you and leave."

"Okay, okay. I get what you're doing," Orthin said before raising his voice. "Please! That's all I have I swear! I'll get the rest... Just give me another day to live! Think of my children!"

"Dial it back a bit. This isn't a Galvetic opera," Jason muttered before standing and raising his own voice. "You have one day...then I kill you."

"Are you still acting?" 701 asked quietly.

"No...I meant that part," Jason said. "Let's go."

Jason had been working his way through the Siblecc Outer Frontier, gathering intel on a Vissalo named Ancula, for the better part of three weeks now. When Lucky and Kage had disappeared from a frontier outpost called The Gates, he had immediately been suspicious that it wasn't some random circumstance. Lucky had worked in that area before as the infamous assassin named Seven and had partnered with a contract broker named Sete Apendi. They had talked to Apendi when they'd first arrived in the region, so the logical assumption was that the slippery Eshquarian had something to do with their disappearance or at least knew who did.

After they'd shut down the Luuxir trafficking rings, Jason and Crusher paid Apendi a little visit. They'd avoided the cagey contractor's plethora of anti-personnel and anti-intrusion traps by crashing in through his ceiling rather than fighting in through a door or window. They were easily able to subdue Apendi, but the old bastard had been tougher than he looked. Crusher went to work on him while Jason forced himself to stay and watch. The amount of pain inflicted on Apendi still gave Jason occasional nightmares. The Eshquarian hadn't survived the interrogation, but they'd at least gotten a name: Ancula. From there, they were able to use their own intel sources and map out a general area of operation and where his ship was known to pop up at from time to time.

His original plan had been to head out alone aboard his Jepsen SX-5. The *Phoenix* had been shot out from under him by a surface-to-orbit gun emplacement that took most of her right wing off and left her stranded on a hostile world. She had been recovered and was now back on S'Tora being overhauled by Twingo and his local crew. Crusher was also out since the moron had convinced Doc to tweak him to arrest, or slightly reverse, his aging. The result was that Crusher was indeed in prime fighting form again...with all the emotional instabilities inherent in Galvetic youth. He was a liability, so he was back on S'Tora with Doc trying to correct things.

Jason had almost been looking forward to heading out alone

despite the danger but, at the last minute, 701 had intercepted him and demanded he be allowed to go along. The battlesynth was a formidable soldier, but he and Jason didn't particularly like each other on a personal level. It made the long flight in a tiny ship somewhat awkward.

"You trust him to come to the ship?" 701 asked as they walked back through the grubby mining outpost town.

"I trust him to come and collect his money," Jason said. "He knows I won't kill or maim him without reason."

"This seems a needlessly risky strategy when we already had him in the alley and could have just brought him with us."

Jason sighed, already tired of the condescension and lectures that were par for the course when working with 701. Besides Lucky, the member of the group he most got along with was 707—or *Tin Man*, as he was now known—but the leader of Lot 700 had decided to leave S'Tora and serve with his son Jacob in one of Earth's Scout Fleet teams. Both Tin Man and Lucky were flexible and understood that situations were fluid. 701 was a stickler for doctrine.

"He'll be there," Jason said. "This environment is give and take. I've let him walk away with a few bruises and saved face, he'll give me much of what he knows."

"But not all."

"Of course not. Orthin is connected to all the major players in the information brokering game in this region, and he knows how to play. We'll get enough intel to move on but not enough to link us back to him if we go after someone powerful and fail."

"And, in the meantime, Lucky and Kage remain captives while we...play games."

Jason sighed again.

"Do not question my motivation for getting my friends back," he said wearily. "This is how it's done in this world. We can't come at them head-on. They'll scatter, go underground, word will get out about us, and we'll never find them. I know you've been a soldier far longer than I've been alive, but please try to believe that I know what I'm doing here."

701 said nothing further as they walked back to the starport, which was nothing more than a disorganized bit of tarmac with a rickety fence around it. The SX-5 was sitting near the edge amongst the other smuggler and merc ships. She was so much smaller than the others that many probably thought she belonged to one of the larger ships sitting in orbit.

So far, the mission had been frustrating and, thanks to 701, annoying. But to be fair, the battlesynth had so far lived up to his end of the deal and was letting Jason work through the underworld to get the intel they needed without too much interference or complaining. How long that would remain was anybody's guess.

"Burke? I'm here."

"I knew you'd do the right thing, Orthin," Jason said, waving him aboard as the ship's sensors scanned him, finding two small holdout blasters hidden in his clothing. "Not too heavily armed, I see."

"You want me to lose them?"

"Don't bother. This is a friendly conversation," Jason said, tossing him the bundle of credit chits. "Here. Didn't even charge you a service fee."

"I figured you'd want some sort of payment for the trouble of almost decapitating me in that alley," Orthin said. "Thanks for that, by the way."

"We can speak freely here. Tell me about Ancula."

"What do you want to know? If you're thinking of jacking one of his shipments, don't. Even with a battlesynth, you'd be signing your own death warrant."

"Nothing like that," Jason waved him off. "I actually don't even need him, just someone who is known to always be around him."

"You're not talking about that crazy synth, Suta, are you?" Orthin asked.

"Maybe," Jason said. "You've heard of him?"

"Oh, yeah. A real sadist, that one. He's not like your quiet friend over there. Not even a real battlesynth, though they sort of have him dressed up like one. What do you want with him?"

"He took something from a client of mine. I'm simply trying to recover it or, barring that, confirm its destruction."

"Not sure I can be much help, Burke. Suta is always around Ancula aboard the *Unjuss*, but he's also deployed as an enforcer from time to time without much warning."

"Anything you have would be appreciated," Jason said, pulling a credit chit out and squeezing it so the display lit up to show it was charged with ten thousand credits. Orthin eyed it hungrily.

"I might have a thing or two I know that would be worth your trouble."

Over the next two hours, Orthin gave them specific information on two of Ancula's operations in the area. By the time he left, he was laughing with Jason like they were old friends and appeared completely at ease as he walked down the ramp and into the night. Jason raised the ramp and started the automated pre-flight on the ship, not wanting to risk staying stationary after letting him leave.

"That was...fascinating," 701 said. "Perhaps I have underestimated you. Your strategy of coming at him obliquely and working toward our target by pretending to be after another is something simple, yet I would have never thought to employ it. Well done. I do not think he suspects he was played for a fool."

"Thanks," Jason said. "But it does raise an interesting question; who is this Suta? Orthin seemed more afraid of him than he did Ancula. You heard of any badass upgraded synths out here raising hell on the frontier?"

"Synths being used in combat is not unheard of, nor is it unusual to see them get involved in criminal enterprises," 701 said. "But there were some specifics about his description that make me uneasy. Would you be averse to me contacting 707 and consulting with him on this matter?"

"Knock yourself out." Jason gestured to the small com station. "I'm going to get us into space and hit the rack for a bit. We can figure out where we're heading next after that."

701 bent over to access the terminal. He was one of the few battlesynths that had spent time around humans that still had an aversion to sitting on furniture. In the weeks they'd been aboard together, the only time he'd seen 701 sit had been when he took a shift in the pilot's seat. All other times, he stood, looming over Jason as he slept, ate, read, or anything else he did in the small ship. Since the SX-5 was modular and mission scalable, he'd been able to have the starport crew back home load her with a full head that included a shower as well as an alcove that was on the port bulkhead that had a comfortable rack and storage for all his gear. Still, there was only so much the designers could do with such a limited amount of real estate, so privacy aboard was practically nonexistent.

"Engines are up," Jason said. "You ready?"

"You may depart at your leisure," 701 said. "It might be some time before I can make contact."

Jason slid into the pilot's seat and, out of habit, almost sent a request for clearance to lift before he remembered this section of the planet was just a free-for-all. He checked his sensors before feeding power to the grav-drive and pulling the small ship smoothly into the air. As soon as he pushed her into a shallow climb away from the field, the computer helpfully retracted the gear and began rigging for exo-atmospheric flight.

He was just transitioning to the thermosphere when alarms blared and the computer highlighted two capital warships dropping down from a transfer orbit that appeared to be on a direct intercept for him. Their beacons identified them as belonging to a military within the Etan System, a place he'd never heard of before. The SX-5 was far enough away he had a few options but, for the moment, he just held his speed and course.

Sure enough, as his ship maintained her climb, the two inbound ships continued to descend, ignoring him completely. He relaxed a bit and continued to monitor them, wondering what they were up to. Ships that big could feasibly land on the surface, but it was such a pain in the ass nobody ever wanted to do it. Even a ship as small as the *Devil's Fortune* took nearly two days to get from a holding orbit down to landing.

"What the hell?" he muttered, glancing at 701 as the battlesynth moved up to look at the tactical displays.

"They are about to attack the surface," he said.

"Absurd," Jason said even as the ships decelerated dramatically and spaced themselves apart, holding in a geostationary position directly over the settlement they'd just left.

Then, they opened fire.

This was no precision strike. Both ships rained down hell onto the surface with full-power salvos from their plasma cannons. Within seconds, the entire area on the planet was engulfed in fire, smoke, and billowing clouds of dust...but still they fired. Jason pushed the SX-5 to full power to clear the area, completely ignoring the protocols on orbital departure and taking a direct line away from the planet.

"What the fuck was that?!"

"I believe we are seeing the beginnings of what will happen in the vacuum of the ConFed's absence," 701 said grimly.

The bombardment went on for a full seven minutes and took out three settlements on that side of the planet before the firing halted and the warships climbed away. As they fled, the lead ship broadcast a message in Jenovian Standard on all local band channels.

"Justice belongs to the people of Etan. Let Antergen see that we are willing to meet force with force and tremble."

"Short, yet useless," Jason muttered, doing a Nexus search for *Antergen* to see if he could gain any context. The local nets had a handful of sources that shed some light on the issue.

"This planet is a Teir-3 vassal world of Antergen Prime. Looks like it isn't used for much more than some light mining and a half-assed colonization effort, but the interesting part is that seventy years or so ago the world had been claimed by Etan-3. The Antergen government petitioned the ConFed and was awarded the planet in a unanimous decision. After that they came and... Ah."

"Yes?" 701 asked.

"Says here they came and sanitized the planet in preparation of their own colonization effort. Basically, they came and wiped out the Etan colonists."

"And they could not retaliate against Antergen because the ConFed fleet stood in the way," 701 said. "As I said...this is the beginning."

The battlesynth went back to the com station as Jason watched the sensor feeds and listened to the local com traffic in horror. With the fall of the ConFed being kept quiet, he'd hoped that most worlds would just assume everything was the same as it had always been. It looked like a few were clearly aware that, unless they attacked a Core World, they were pretty much able to do as they pleased.

He'd certainly been no fan of the corrupt ConFed with its author-itarian tendencies and abuses of lower tier worlds, but there had to be an alternative to what he had just witnessed and had almost gotten caught up in. If Orthin had been a few hours later to collect his money...

3

"I will kill you!"

The rage-filled shout was followed by a bestial roar that shook the windows in the lab.

"You're only making this take longer than necessary," a voice said over the intercom. "You can't break the straps, Crusher, so settle down and let the serum do its work."

"Fuck you, you blue-skinned shit weasel! I'll tear your head off!"

"I almost forgot how unpleasant he was when he was younger," Twingo said, peering through the window. "You're sure he can't break the restraints?"

"Positive," Doc said.

"What about the anchor points on the table the straps are attached to?" Twingo asked.

"Uh," Doc said, looking in through the window. "Pretty sure."

"And this is supposed to do what, exactly?"

"I'm adjusting his hormone levels," Doc said. "The initial treatment had an...unexpected result. His age regression put him into what the Galvetics call a transitory period where aggression and anger responses are off the charts. I need to get him back on the other side of that."

"In other words, you're tinkering with things you don't fully understand," Twingo said, still watching Crusher try to rip the heavy straps from the table.

"I... Mistakes were made," Doc sighed. "In my hubris, I leapt at the chance to work on a Galvetic warrior given the centuries of secrecy surrounding their breeding program. Not only did I find that they had been lying the entire time, but I also had to accept the fact that my time being on this crew has dulled my skill and instincts as a geneticist."

"Well...if you're going to recklessly experiment, at least you did it with one of the most dangerous species in the galaxy. So, good job there."

On the table, the serum and the drugs Doc had administered took hold, and Crusher's head fell back onto the table with a loud *thud*, and his eyes rolled back into his head. The sensors monitoring his vitals indicated that he'd finally fallen into a deep sleep.

Doc deeply regretted what he had done. Crusher had come to him after a particularly harrowing mission in which he hadn't been able to keep up with Jason and Lucky. He felt like a liability, so he wanted Doc to *tweak* him like he had Jason. The big warrior wanted his strength and youth back. Who wouldn't?

At first, he'd turned Crusher down, worried about his ability to even do the job without a proper staff and time to research. Jason had been relatively simple. He'd had a whole team on the task, and the human body readily took to the enhancements. But Crusher had been persistent and pathetically sincere. He only wanted the ability to protect his friends, he'd said. Doc relented and began the initial work ups and consulted with the Archive—a super AI named Voq—to develop a treatment plan. That had taken him down a dark and dangerous path.

What they found was that the highly secretive Galvetic selective breeding program the empire claimed developed the warrior caste was all a lie. Galvetic warriors had been created by a genetic manipulation program whose fingerprints were all over Crusher's DNA. The work was good. Subtle. But it had also been done generations ago, and the Galvetics couldn't imagine a system as powerful as Voq would tear their work down to the foundation to learn what they had done. It was a secret the Galvetic Empire would kill over. Not even Crusher, the Guardian Archon and veritable royalty, would be safe from their assassin teams if they learned what Doc had done.

Now, Jason had disappeared with the SX-5 without a word, Lucky and Kage were missing, Twingo was busy trying to rebuild the *Phoenix* as fast as he could, and Doc was left holding the bag trying to stabilize Crusher's condition *and* come up with a plan to handle the coming political fallout from the Galvetic Empire. So far, he'd come up with exactly nothing.

"You ever think about reaching out to the Reddix brothers?" Twingo asked, seeming to read his thoughts. "Or at least Mazer?"

"What good would that do?" Doc asked. "We're trying to hide this from the legions not invite them here to kill Crusher...although that would simplify things a bit."

"Mazer can be trusted," Twingo said. "I can talk to him for you, but I won't without your permission."

"This final serum should work," Doc said. "Crusher will be out of the danger zone and ready to begin full rehabilitation. After that, it will be difficult to keep him hidden on S'Tora. He'll want to go after Jason and the others, which means the risk of him being discovered goes up exponentially."

"I'm well aware of all that."

"Ask him to come. Be discreet about it but tell him we need to see him—and *only* him—at the Archon's request."

"I'll handle it. I'll ask 784 to come with a few friends to make sure the conversation stays civil," Twingo said, rising to leave.

"Not 701?"

"They're not saying, but I'm pretty sure 701 went with Jason."

"Oh... Those two don't really like each other all that much, and there's no getting away inside the SX-5," Doc said. "Thanks for telling me. I actually feel better now."

"No charge," Twingo said. "Glad I stopped by to see *that* one raging like a moron, but I need to get back to the base. We're ready to bring the main reactor back online and begin initial system checks."

"You needed to see me?"

"We have a problem. Big problem." Mazer Reddix stood at the window of his office overlooking the pristine grounds of the Galvetic Legions Special Detachment Operations Center. It was the home base of the planet Restaria of Galvetic special forces, including the vaunted and feared Zeta-Saka.

"*We?*" Morakar Reddix asked. "I'm semi-retired."

"It's about Felex," Mazer said.

"Dead?"

"Worse."

"How is that possible?"

"He's...done something. Something that will cause our overseers to order Zeta-Saka teams deployed to hunt him down and kill him," Mazer said.

"He broke the covenant?" Morakar asked, referring to the ancient pact between the warrior caste and Galvator.

"It's about on par with that." Mazer gestured to the com panel in the far wall. "Go ahead and tell him, Twingo. This room is secure."

"Hello, Morakar," Omega Force's engineer said through the speakers. "Sorry to be reaching out under these circumstances."

Over the next two hours, Twingo described what Jovren Ma'Fredich and Felex Tezakar—Doc and Crusher—had done. As he went on, Mazer watched the growing horror Morakar was experiencing written all over his face.

"How noticeable is the change?" he asked once Twingo finished his story.

"Too much to hide. I know you guys age well for the most part, but he looks about as young as when I first met him," Twingo said.

"This is bad," Morakar said.

"There's more," Twingo warned. "And it pertains to all of you, but I'd rather tell you in person. Better yet, I'd rather Doc told you."

"What are you asking of us?" Mazer turned from the window.

"I'm not really sure," Twingo admitted. "I'm not trying to dump this in your lap but, obviously, my concern is for Crusher's future... mostly that he has one."

"I feel my brother and I will need to discuss this further in private, Twingo," Morakar said. "We will contact you once we reach some sort of decision. I appreciate you bringing this directly to us and being so open."

"Yeah...no problem," Twingo said, sounding disappointed. "I'll let Doc know I spoke to you."

Once the connection was terminated, Mazer stared at his brother expectantly.

"I already know where you stand on this," Morakar said. "But if we're caught helping him or even concealing this from the Imperial Legate, our lives are forfeit. Our family name disgraced and stricken from the records. This is no time for rash decisions, Mazer."

"He is the Guardian Archon and—"

"And he has violated a sacred trust! No matter how noble his intentions, the reality of what he has done cannot be just swept away because you still harbor your boyhood worship of the Archon! He has spit in *all* our faces!"

Mazer said nothing. He looked away in disgust as his older brother struggled to compose himself. Morakar had always been the better of them. Honorable to a fault and one who adhered strictly to their code and his oath. Even for a friend such as Felex, there was no room for exception. His brother wasn't heartless, he simply had a higher degree of discipline than Mazer ever would. If one knew him well enough, they would see that the news of Felex's betrayal had hurt Morakar deeply.

"What will you do?" he finally asked.

"I...don't know," Morakar said. "My duty and oath demand that I report this immediately...but my loyalty to my brother is stopping me."

"Perhaps you're right, and I am emotionally compromised in this issue," Mazer said. "Too much to be counted on to do the right thing. Since we were children, your judgment has been unerring. You've never led us astray before, and I don't think you'll do so now. I will abide by and support whatever decision you make, Morakar."

"You trusted me to share in this secret," Morakar said. "Let us take a short time to reflect on this separately. After that, we will decide together how best to proceed."

"I appreciate this. Truly."

Morakar left, and Mazer went back to his brooding at the window. His brother was absolutely right. Felex—Crusher—might have done this out of a misguided sense of loyalty to Jason Burke, but he had an obligation to his own people as well, and he betrayed that. It was difficult to know how he should feel about that.

4

"Damn! This place reeks."

Jason stood at the bottom of the SX-5's ramp, shivering in the early morning chill, the ship's engines popping and pinging as they cooled. They were on a moon called Haziev Minor. Orthin had told them that rumors were circulating that Ancula was searching for something. Others said that he'd found it but had no way to get to it. Jason and 701 figured if they could find out what he was after, maybe even get to it first, then he would have to deal with them for Lucky and Kage.

"Sulfur mines to the west," 701 said. "I imagine it is quite unpleasant for you."

"But not you?" Jason asked.

"I can analyze atmospheric composition, but I do not *smell* the air as you think of it."

"Let's get moving," Jason said, slipping his helmet on. "From what Orthin said, this broker doesn't stay in once place for very long."

The gravity on Haziev Minor was uncomfortably low, but not so light that he was bouncing as he walked. Like all small, light gravity worlds, it also had a thinner atmosphere than he was used to so he was forced to wear his helmet so he could breathe normally. One added benefit was that he could command it to filter out the sulfur particles completely.

The moon had originally been like nearly every other frontier outpost: a logistics hub for the big mining corporations that had the capital and motivation to push the edges of known space and discover new star systems with exploitable resources. The Haziev System was an odd case because both habitable planets, Haziev-2 and Haziev-4, have indigenous populations of intelligent beings that were in the pre-agricultural, pre-industrial stages respectively. The planets were off-limits, but there were three habitable moons orbiting Haziev-3, a Class II gas giant. The three mining companies interested in prospecting in the outer system petitioned the ConFed to use Haziev Minor as a base of operations and, after paying enough in bribes and fees, were granted clearance.

The prospecting turned up nothing worth moving in a major harvesting operation, so the mining companies pulled out, venture capitalists and criminals moved in. There was never any shortage of demand for worlds that slipped between the cracks of regional governmental oversight. Haziev Minor would eventually be settled and developed by a unique, niche criminal element known as the currency cartels. They were groups that had figured out ways to exploit the banking system and constantly fluctuating exchange rates to their favor. They operated in the thin gray area between legal and illegal and were difficult to pin down so, for the most part, they were left to their own devices. So long as they didn't cause too much trouble, most governments didn't see them worth pursuing.

"The supply chain issues alone would seem to make operating on this world not worth the hassle," 701 said as they stepped onto the open-air streetcar, the main source of local transportation in that particular city.

"Depends on what you're looking for," Jason said. "The quadrant is entering a state of upheaval and uncertainty now that the ConFed has collapsed. Small, useless worlds like this that are too far away from anything important will largely be spared. As long as they can keep the shipments coming, they can just wait it out."

"Perhaps," 701 said.

The contact they were looking for was someone Orthin had told them helped Ancula finance things he wanted kept off the books, even from his own organization. This person might be able to at least point them in the right direction. It was a long shot, but the other tip they'd received from the information broker was high-risk, and Jason wasn't ready to expose their involvement this early in the game. He hoped to recover his friends without having to shoot his way out given how low on resources he was. No Crusher, no *Phoenix*...just one arrogant battlesynth and the hope that Lucky would still be combat effective when he tracked them down.

The ride was pleasant and the car, while somewhat dated, was well-maintained and clean much like the rest of the city they were riding through. He noticed that the syndicates that specialized in financial or political criminal enterprise lived in much nicer areas than your average drug or gun runner. Then, of course, you had the bottom rung scum like the traffickers and slavers. The city appeared to be no more than half a century old and, if one didn't know better, they might think it was an enclave of the wealthy who had built their own community to get away from the less desirables.

"Next one," he said, hitting the button on the arm rest to signal the car he wanted it to stop. It dutifully chimed and began braking.

"Standby for next stop, Roella Square," a voice came from speakers near the headrests. "Next stop, Roella Square."

701 created a bit of a stir when he stood, which then led to them looking away quickly as Jason followed. They likely assumed the battlesynth was his personal bodyguard, and anyone who could afford that wasn't someone you wanted to get caught staring at. Once they were on the walkway, the streetcar smoothly rolled away, and Jason took a moment to get his bearings.

They walked one block up, and then two blocks south until they were standing in front of a narrow three-story building made of natural stone and large, arched windows. He scanned the building in multiple wavelengths through the helmet's sensors and detected a few obvious anti-intrusion measures and some hidden weapon systems, but nothing that should cause them any real worry. The fact they were so easily found made him think there were probably more potent measures he couldn't see.

"Here goes nothing," he said, pressing a call button on the gate post in front of the stairs leading up to the entrance.

"Who are you two supposed to be?" a voice asked.

"I was told by an intara named Orthin that you were someone I should speak to about a little problem I have," Jason said.

"That seems unlikely. Where is Orthin now?"

"We should talk about that in private," Jason said, reaching into his pocket and pulling two platinum bars out and waving them in front of the camera so that the certification stamps showed. "I can make it worth your time."

"Wow. Two whole bars."

"Obviously, there's more where that came from. That shit is heavy, and I don't carry it around on me in public."

"You're walking around with battlesynth muscle, and you're worried about getting robbed?"

"You can stop stalling. You're not going to find us in any database no matter how long you search. At least not with a quick and dirty security scan and no valid voiceprint," Jason said, his helmet randomly modulating his voice in a thousand small, subtle ways that would make pinpointing him impossible. "We're not with any government."

"Says you."

"Would I be wasting my time, exposed, if I had the authority of a planetary government to just have my partner blast your door out of the frame and come in after you?"

"Fair point. Just so you know, I have my own security as well."

"I'd expect no less. We're just here to talk, and what we have to talk about doesn't even directly involve you."

"You're not going away until I do?"

"Nope."

"Fine. Come around the back. You definitely don't want to walk through that front door."

"We are trusting him?" 701 asked as they walked down the alley to the rear of the building.

"No. But it's not like we'll convince him to come outside to meet with us," Jason said. "Either we risk speaking to him on his own turf or we go with Plan B, which you didn't like and the reason we're here in the first place."

"Please, stop right there," the voice of the host said once they were at the back of the building.

"We are being scanned," 701 said.

"Lose the helmet and the weapons. I don't suppose the battlesynth would consider waiting outside?"

"No chance at all," 701 said. "But I will keep my weapons powered down and stowed the entire time."

"Fair enough. Human, huh? Interesting. Come on up." A door slid open at the top of a short staircase. Jason and 701 exchanged a look, and the battlesynth took the lead. While he might not have been overly fond of Jason, he didn't view him as expendable, so there was at least that.

"Introductions?"

"My name is Jason Burke. This is Combat Unit 701."

"You may call me Abrus."

Abrus was a Veran, which wasn't a surprise. The species seemed to naturally gravitate to any endeavor that dealt in real-time, complex data handling whether that enterprise was legal or not. What was unusual was that Abrus wasn't green like Kage and every other Veran Jason had ever met. He had red skin and was taller and bulkier.

Jason knew that this particular race of Veran lived in the extreme northern regions of Ver in much smaller communities than their green-hued cousins. They also didn't leave their home planet very often, so he had never actually met one in person.

"Abrus, thank you for taking this meeting."

"What is this, a corporate meet and greet? Get to the point. I only let you in because of the attention you were drawing milling around on the front walkway," Abrus said. "But tell me, how is Orthin these days?"

"Dead," Jason said bluntly. "The planet we were on was hit from orbit over some regional dispute. Orthin was still on the surface as far as I know."

"That's a shame. He owed me quite a bit of money and, instead, all I get is you two. Okay...spit it out. What can Abrus do for you today?"

"We're here about a Vissalo named Ancula," Jason said.

"Ah. Well, in that case, you can get up and take your ass right back out the door you came in through," Abrus stood and turned to leave.

"That would be unwise," 701 said calmly, his eyes snapping red with a harsh *pop* and the whine of charging weapons. Abrus froze.

"You promised," he accused.

"If you leave now, I consider our agreement nullified. Please, sit. Hear the captain out, then make your decision."

"I'm sure you've scanned the room. You know you're sitting in a hardened dome full of explosives. You should also know that there's a dead man's switch rigged to my neural implant. I die, you die," Abrus said.

"But what about a simple maiming?" Jason asked. "If he blows an arm or two off, what then?" He knew Verans well enough to see that Abrus hadn't considered that possibility before.

"This is so uncivilized," Abrus said, sitting back down. "Let's start over, shall we?"

"Let's," Jason said.

"In our newfound spirit of cooperation, I must tell you that if you think I'll help you steal from Ancula, you're insane. You might as well kill me now."

"Steal? I thought your con was ripping off currency exchanges?"

"It's quite a bit more sophisticated than that, but to answer the question, there is a lot that can be done to hide money in much the same way there is to make it. It's all just manipulating the exchange rate and exploiting timing gaps."

"We're not trying to rip off Ancula," Jason said. "You ever hear of an associate of his named Suta?"

"I try not to." Abrus shuddered.

"We're looking for him not Ancula. We just know the two are rarely away from each other, and tracking the higher profile target simplifies our job."

"What did Suta do?"

"Not important. Let's just say he took something from our client, and they would like it back," Jason said, warming up to the lie he'd used on Orthin. Apparently, Ancula was a big enough fish in this pond that nobody would dare cross him, but there appeared to be no love for this Suta character. Abrus seemed to consider this before answering.

"Although I despise Suta, he is still a valuable asset to Ancula. If I helped you take him off the board, my punishment would be no different than if I gave you Ancula himself," he said.

"If it helps, we're only interested in retrieving what was taken. There is no contract on Suta's life, and we don't do freebies," Jason said. "It sounds like killing him would put us at odds with this Ancula, and that's bad for business."

"Fair point, but it doesn't change anything."

"What would it take to change things?" Jason asked.

"To start, I would need to know exactly what you're after. It might not even be something I can give. After that, maybe we can talk price," Abrus said. Jason looked at 701 and shrugged.

"We got word from Orthin that Ancula was mounting an operation he was keeping off the books, even from his own organization. He would need capital of the untraceable sort to pull this off. When we asked, we were told that you would be one of the brokers he might contract to launder the funds and put them where they need to be. If we can figure out when, where, and what this secret operation of his is, we have a solid chance of intercepting Suta."

"Oh, is that all?" Abrus scoffed. "I hate to break it to you, but I handle a lot of transactions for a lot of people. They don't tell me what they're for."

"Give me a break," Jason snorted. "There's no way you don't have some idea what Ancula is after. You might not have all the specific details, but you know something."

"Even if I did, what's in it for me?" Abrus asked. Jason just smiled.

There it was.

The information that Abrus had was for sale, just as Jason knew it would be. But he couldn't just come out and offer it for a price given the nature of his clientele. The trick had been to string him along just enough so that he was convinced what he was selling wouldn't actually come back to bite him in the ass.

"I'm not sure what someone like you would be interested in for trade," Jason said, knowing what he had to offer was something a broker like Abrus would jump at.

"You won't know until you offer. I will tell you this: It had better be something rare and priceless if you want me to consider giving up what you're asking for," Abrus said.

"You ever heard of a Veran named Weef Zadra?"

"Of course, but she's long gone, so what's your point?"

"She's gone...her intelligence network is not. Some few people still have ways to access it, one of those people being me."

"You're offering me Weef Zadra's network?"

"I'm offering you an opportunity to use it for a short span of time," Jason corrected. "No restrictions on what you search for."

"This isn't some sort of con? I'll know what I'm looking at. You can't fool me."

"Why would I waste my time with that? You interested or not?"

"I'm listening."

5

"See? No problem."

"Other than the principle of unintended consequences."

"What's that supposed to mean?" Jason demanded.

"Only that you provided access to one of the quadrant's most powerful intelligence networks for over two hours to someone of ill repute," 701 said. "We cannot be certain what he intends to do with the information he has gleaned."

"We know what he searched. The interface wasn't quite as secure as he thought it was. Voq designed the thing to be damn near uncrackable. Abrus was wanting information on Khepri's phase four plans for the expansion of the banking system now that the Pillar Worlds are withdrawing and forming their own nation."

"Why would he want that information?"

"Since stealing and laundering money in the narrow gaps of currency transactions is what he does, I'm assuming he needs to have a heads up on what's planned that could make his life difficult," Jason said. "You worry too much."

"And you not nearly enough."

"I get that a lot."

Abrus had folded quickly once he realized Jason had been serious and was offering him access to the Zadra Network, as it was now known. Jason had been given back door access into the system, which was now maintained by Earth, as payment for services rendered when he'd helped his son take out the head of the One World faction threatening to destabilize Earth's government. Jason had gladly taken part in the operation given that One World's leader, Margaret Jansen, had tried to have him killed once.

The network wasn't quite as powerful as it had been when Weef Zadra herself had run it, and Earth had let it fall into disrepair as they didn't fully understand how to maintain such a fragile, amorphous thing. Jason had stepped in once again and used his access to the system to let Voq—the Archive—begin rebuilding all the interconnecting threads to all the individual assets. The hyper-advanced AI also helpfully gave Jason deeper hooks into the system and bolstered its internal security protocols to limit the chance of it falling into the wrong hands.

"Do you think the information we received in return is valid?" 701 asked.

"Undoubtedly. You see how exposed he is here. He won't risk us coming back," Jason said. "Oh, sure...this isn't everything he knows. It's just enough to get him what he wanted and make sure we fly away forever."

"I can see the logic in that assessment," 701 said grudgingly.

"Let's get to the ship and get airborne so we can have a look at this," Jason said, patting where the datacard sat in his pocket.

"You no longer like sitting on a planet longer than necessary," 701 said. It wasn't a question.

"Between you and me? That orbital attack we almost got caught up in has me spooked," Jason said. "I've been out here for... Hell I don't even know how many years now. I've never seen something like that happen without plenty of advance warning."

"The experience was...jarring," 701 admitted.

The SX-5 zipped along toward her mesh-out point while Jason and 701 pored over the data Abrus had provided them.

It wasn't much.

"Do you understand these transaction codes?" Jason asked.

"Some," 701 said. "When our master decided to hide Lot 700, he needed to move capital from slush accounts within the Ministry of Martial Affairs, specifically the Battlesynth Program Office, to private holding accounts so that he could build the subterranean holding facility you found us in. Myself and 784 were involved with that."

"Anything leaping out at you?"

The data was nothing but a series of move orders that Ancula had told Abrus to execute. The orders took funds from hundreds of accounts across Ancula's organization and funneled them into three different accounts. It was clever having Abrus handle the transfers. What the Veran was able to do was siphon off a little at a time over a course of weeks just before the accounts had their automated maintenance cycles where balances are adjusted by Khepri to reflect the change in currency values compared to the Standard Credit. To the casual eye, it would look completely ordinary that values would fluctuate or even trend downward on accounts across various worlds.

"Let us ignore where the funding was coming from. That is irrelevant," 701 said. "We can just assume he is pulling from so many accounts because he wishes this to remain hidden. By focusing on the amounts and the destination accounts, we can begin to put together a clearer picture of what he might be after."

"You think the money is still in those three accounts, or were these a pass-through to someplace else?" Jason asked.

"Relevant question," 701 said. "Do you know anybody who would be able to trace the movement out of these accounts?"

"I could reach out and see," Jason said. "The people who do this sort of work tend to not stick around in one place too long. Normally, I would just have Kage handle it, but that's not an option right now."

"We will get them back," 701 said. "For now, let us see if we can at least trace these three accounts to their places of origin and begin working the problem from that point."

"That should be simple enough," Jason said, turning back to the terminal.

The Zadra Network wasn't really designed to handle queries like tracking down individual account holders, but it did have enough hooks into the financial sector to run it back to where the accounts were issued. Most of those functions were automated and wouldn't need to be handled by a live asset. The return came barely five minutes later.

"Sepura Prime. Bank of Pikengren. All three accounts are serviced there."

"That is a Core World," 701 said, leaning over to read the information.

"Figures," Jason muttered, opening a new screen and punching in the new data. "Almost a nine-day flight if I really push her."

"Do you think it would be advantageous to go there personally?" 701 asked. "They will not likely give us anything useful."

"A Core World bank would be sensitive to any sort of investigation from the Kheprian authorities, wouldn't it?"

"To put it mildly," 701 said. "But you are not Kheprian."

"You are," Jason pointed out.

"Okay, then neither of us are pru. Khepri doesn't send battlesynths to do a bureaucrat's job."

"I think this is still workable," Jason said. "Let me get in touch with some people but, in the meantime, go ahead and get us flying toward the Sepura System."

"You wish to be flying toward a target before you even have a plan firmly in your mind, much less ready to execute?"

"Yep."

"As I have noted before, I am not sure how you have survived as long as you have."

"How'd she do?"

"I'm quite pleased," Twingo said, straightening as Doc walked into the empty hangar. "Definitely will need to tweak and tune her but, overall, the new propulsion management system worked like a charm. How is your project?"

"He's stable. I've got him up and about," Doc said.

"You left him alone?"

"Nope. We had guests arrive this morning, which is why I'm here to see you. Where *is* the ship, by the way?"

"She's at the farm. Two of the battlesynths are finishing up some last-minute things on her for me, and I'm taking the opportunity to clean up in here. Once that's done, we can—" The sound of multiple vehicles pulling up outside the main gate to the complex made Twingo pause and walk toward the doors to look out. What he saw made him frown.

"Those vehicles are marked as federal authorities. That's planetary enforcement," Doc said. "What did you do?"

"Nothing!" Twingo said. "The testing program wasn't done on S'Tora."

"Please, open the gate. We will not ask twice," a voice boomed from the lead vehicle.

"Better comply for now," Doc said.

Twingo went to the control panel and hit the button to open the main gate. As soon as it rolled halfway back, seven vehicles came roaring up the drive, across the landing pad, and right into the hangar.

"I don't like this at all," he said as armed S'Torans climbed out. They didn't brandish their weapons, but they were held at the ready.

"I am looking for Jason Burke," another S'Toran with the stench of government bureaucrat said, walking forward.

"Off-world," Twingo said.

"And you are?"

"We're employees of Mr. Burke and not citizens of S'Tora," Doc said. "May I ask what this is about?"

"This is about a new zero tolerance policy on S'Tora for harboring certain lawless elements. Mr. Burke has been identified as running an illegal paramilitary operation out of this base."

"There's nothing illegal about it. The company is a licensed security provider registered on—"

"Niceen-3...yes, we're aware of that," the official said. "That bit of technicality doesn't change the fact Mr. Burke is running a mercenary company off of our planet. I have a binding order from the regional magistrate that says this property, these facilities, and anything on or in them belongs to the government of S'Tora. We have seized his bank accounts as well. Now...where is the ship that is usually here?"

"I assume it is also off-world with Mr. Burke." Twingo shrugged. "I'm just the janitor, and he's a facility supervisor."

"You will not interfere with my people as they search the premises."

"Wouldn't dream of it," Twingo said. "We'll just stand out there?" He pointed toward the landing pad.

"That will be fine. Just know that once we leave, we will be sealing the gates, and the property will be off limits with guards posted until the government decides what to do with it."

"You mind me asking what has prompted all this?" Doc asked. "Burke has had an understanding with the S'Toran government for some years now."

"He has had an arrangement with the local government, which is not the same thing. With the ConFed gone, new directives are coming down to eliminate any potential threats to the planet. S'Tora will remain entirely neutral in any and all regional conflicts. Now, please step outside."

"This is bad," Doc said once they were out of earshot. "They're really taking the base."

Twingo said nothing as he walked out the door and over to a smaller building that backed up against the edge of the mountain the base was carved into. He slipped inside and went to what looked like a normal electrical junction box, yanking it open and pressing his palm to a biometric reader while holding down a red button with his other hand. A second later, there was a double *beep*."

"We need to go. Now," Twingo said, walking over to the 1967 Camaro convertible that Jason kept stored there when he was away.

"What did you do?"

"That's the emergency purge I installed last year. I just fried our entire mainframe inside the hangar, all the com nodes...everything. I also just sent out a general alert to about a dozen of our dead drop addresses to not come back here."

Twingo slid into the driver's seat and adjusted the seat while Doc climbed in next to him.

"This is hardly a subtle vehicle," he said.

"No choice," Twingo said. "Besides, they don't seem to be too worried about us, just looting our base. All our spare parts for the *Phoenix*, spare munitions, the armory...all gone."

"The captain always warned us about getting too comfortable putting down roots," Doc said.

"Yeah," Twingo turned the key and the big V8 roared to life. "He'll be so happy he was proven right."

The red muscle car shot out of the building and hauled ass up the road away from the hanger. Twingo looked in the mirrors and saw that two of the troops had come running out to see what the noise was, and then ran back inside.

"Might have company. Is this thing fast?" Doc asked. Twingo smiled and shifted into fourth gear before smashing the throttle.

"Should be plenty to keep ahead of the ground cars they use around here," he said. "It's a damn good thing I decided to leave the ship at the farm. Talk about dumb luck."

"We're going to need to evac," Doc said. "All of it. The battlesynths will need to get the *Devil's Fortune* prepped for flight and the hell out of here. If they figure out those businesses are owned by Jason's holding company, they'll seize them as well."

"What a mess," Twingo said, the reality of the blow they'd just been dealt sinking into the pit of his stomach. "So...who were our visitors?"

"Huh? Oh," Doc said. "The Reddix brothers flew in from Restaria. Arrived this morning."

"You realize they're probably here to kill Crusher, right?"

"They swore they were not."

"Where should we go first?"

"Go to the lab complex," Doc said as he craned his head around to see if they were being pursued. "We'll talk with Mazer and Morakar and see what they think we should do with Crusher, and then get to the *Phoenix* and get her off-world."

"I'll drop you and continue on myself to the ship. You have a different vehicle I can take?" Twingo asked.

"Yeah. The facility has a fleet of ground cars available for use, but they can be tracked. Do you really want to take one of those straight to the farm and cause them to start poking around there too hard?"

"You have a point. I'll just head straight there and try to stash this thing. You get Crusher ready to move, and then contact me with the plan. Ideally, you need to come to me. I don't want to risk flying her from there to here, and then a climb to orbit."

"We'll figure out something," Doc said. "Just get her prepped and tell the battlesynths they need to get the Archive out of here. We'll try and find safe harbor for them somewhere else."

"This really turned to shit on us quick," Twingo said. "First we lose Lucky and Kage, then Crusher goes crazy—your fault, by the way—and now we're getting booted from our home."

"It might be a little worse than that," Doc said. "How many of the Omega Force operational accounts were based here on S'Tora?"

"Shit! We're poor, too!" Twingo wailed.

"There are emergency funds stashed around, and we still have the treasure haul from the Luuxir trafficking ring we took...but those will take time to access, and the *Phoenix* doesn't run on hopes and dreams," Doc said.

"Let's just get her into space, the hell away from here, and we'll deal with that," Twingo said. "Damn. What a mess."

"What if we are engaged and this pack takes enemy fire?" Lucky asked.

"Then, it was nice knowing you."

"What if I'm standing near you when it happens?"

"It's directional and contained."

"Even if it breaches my power core?"

"Enough!" Suta shouted. "Stay here until they finish the adjustments, and then you have two hours to see your little friend before mission planning starts."

Suta stomped out of the bay, his head making uncontrolled twitches, and he muttered aloud to himself.

"A word of advice?" one of the techs asked.

"Speak," Lucky said.

"Don't go out of your way to anger that one. He has killed people for less, and Master Ancula lets him for some reason."

"I am well acquainted with him. He was no better a century ago."

"I'm sorry, but I can't disable this device for you," the tech said. "I've set a logic delay that shouldn't be too obvious, but if they're determined to kill you, it will go off."

"I appreciate your efforts, but please do not put yourself at undue risk on my account. My name is Lucky."

"I'm Saf Rifi. My friend over there just goes by Welg."

"If I am ready, I will leave you two to your work. It was nice meeting you."

"You as well," Saf said. "Be careful around here. You don't seem like the usual sort that gets...recruited. They're apparently afraid enough of you to have us go through all this"—he gestured to the explosive pack—"so I assume you can handle yourself, but they are especially ruthless."

"I understand," Lucky said.

Now that he had an explosive device attached to control him, he was allowed to move about the ship in the areas Suta had designated as authorized. The conversation with the engineering techs was illuminating. Apparently, not even the crew of Ancula's ship were all here willingly if he was reading the subtext correctly. He wasn't sure how he might use that to his advantage, but it was certainly something to keep in mind.

He was ushered into the infirmary without issue and found Kage in much better shape than the last time Lucky had seen him. The Veran was back to his normal, healthy green color, and his eyes were bright and animated. He was also restrained to the bed.

"You can speak freely," Kage said. "The room isn't being monitored."

"That seems unlikely," Lucky said.

"Well, it was. But the system is on the fritz for some reason." Kage winked at him. "Nice backpack."

"It is full of explosives. It is supposed to keep me compliant."

"That's what I figured. You meet any of the crew yet?"

"The engineering and armory crew appear to be conscripts. At least some of them," Lucky said.

"Same with the medical staff. Practically everyone here seems to be here against their will. That sound like a practical way to run a crew?"

"If you do not want to pay for quality crewmembers, it can be," Lucky said. "Ancula's original play for Seven revolved around the mimic function. Now that they know it is gone, they are apparently going to try and utilize me in some other way."

"Is this something you can turn to our advantage?" Kage asked.

"Unlikely. Now that his original plan is no longer viable, Ancula seems eager to be rid of us both. Are they going to let you out of this infirmary any time soon?"

"Oh, I'm fine," Kage said. "I've been playing it up to stay here on purpose, and the medical staff has been helping me by pretending to believe me."

"To what purpose?"

"Unsecured network access." Kage gestured to the silvery string of nanites that were coming from his palm and must be interfacing with a network connection somewhere in the room.

"No unnecessary risks," Lucky warned. "At least not yet."

"Can you get a message to the guys?"

"My burst transmitter is still operational but, at the moment, there is nothing to report. I will reach out when there is some way they can actually help."

"We've never had one of these little side adventures, have we? Just you and me? This might end up being fun."

"Do you have anything else to report? If you have disabled surveillance and are actively slicing into their network, we probably shouldn't be spending too much time together," Lucky said.

"Probably not a bad idea. Try to hog most of the attention from Ancula and his pet synth. The longer they ignore me as some harmless, injured Veran, the better for us both."

"I can do that."

Twingo was not a fan of wheeled transportation. He certainly wasn't much of a driver when it came to the antique auto Jason had such an inexplicable fondness for. It was loud, dangerous, and didn't handle particularly well compared to the modern vehicles available. Jason had tried to explain that a car (as he called it) was more than just a way to get around. He claimed it was something his people were passionate about and took great pride in. On Twingo's home planet, hardly anybody actually owned a ground vehicle. Instead, they were just taken from a pool for a fee.

"At least the farm is just ahead," he muttered.

The car's rubber tires squealed around another turn as Twingo fought with the gear shift to get it down into second. There was a grinding from the transmission before it went into gear but, by then, Twingo had let the car slow to the point that it almost stalled. He smashed the throttle to the floor, and the engine responded with a bellowing roar that made him flinch. The rear tires broke loose under the onslaught of torque, and the Camaro fishtailed wildly around the turn.

Twingo, too focused on sawing at the steering wheel, never took his foot off the throttle. Every move he made with the wheel worsened his troubles until he spun the car completely. It slid off the road and onto the damp grasses that were around the entrance to the farm. He slid down the hill, completely out of control, and did two full, lazy rotations before he made it to the tree line, smashing into a large *azuzaco* tree with the front of the car. Sheet metal buckled, and steam erupted from under the damaged hood as the engine spluttered and died.

Shaking off the impact, Twingo undid the restraint belt and climbed up and out of the car as the door was jammed closed. He looked over the damage and cringed. If Jason got pissed about Crusher leaving fingerprints on the car, he could only imagine what he'd say once he saw this.

"Mr. Jason! Are you okay!"

Twingo turned toward the shouting voice and saw Ertz, the coffee farm's production manager, climbing out of a small utility vehicle.

"It's me, Ertz...and, yeah, I think I'm okay."

"Mr. Twingo! Are you angry at Mr. Jason? Is this why you destroy his prize car by crashing into his favorite tree?"

"This is his favorite tree?" Twingo asked skeptically.

"Yes."

"You mean Jason Burke? That guy? He has a favorite tree?"

"Yes."

"Ertz, I've been on the man's crew for years. He's not sentimental. What's so special about this tree?"

"I could not say," Ertz shrugged, "but I know he will be very angry you did this to his car."

"It was an accident, I assure you," Twingo said. "Listen, have you had any visits from some government types? Maybe someone poking around asking about the holding companies?"

"Nothing," Ertz shook his head. "What is happening?"

"S'Tora is revoking their hospitality. They just seized the hangar base, froze Jason's accounts here, and will likely be moving to take his home next."

"Does he still have anything important there?" Ertz asked. "We can go immediately and get it before the authorities do."

"The house is clean," Twingo said. "Jason moved everything important aboard the ship the battlesynths have been protecting. The beach house was just a hangout."

"This is good," Ertz said. "Is that where you are going? To the ship? I can give you a ride."

"I appreciate that," Twingo said, rubbing his neck. He looked back at the still steaming Camaro and shook his head. "Favorite tree, huh?"

When Ertz pulled up to the landing field and concealment structure Jason had had built for the *Devil's Fortune*, the battlesynths were already hard at work. The hardshell cover had been retracted, and everything already moved out and away from the ship in preparation to launch. He could also see that the corvette was running on her own power, so they were very nearly ready to depart. The *Phoenix*, sitting in her new matte black color scheme, was also being readied by Lot 700.

"Twingo, we will be ready for uplift in less than an hour," a battlesynth said as it walked up to the vehicle. Twingo wasn't as familiar with the members of Lot 700 as Jason, so he couldn't tell all the subtle differences between individuals, but he believed he was speaking to 755. He would be the one serving as interim commander when 701 and Tin Man were not around.

"Have you picked a destination yet?" he asked.

"Not yet. Voq is producing a flight path that will look random but allow us to stay out of known trouble spots and not burn an excessive amount of fuel."

"Good," Twingo said. "The hyperlink equipment Earth gave us is all integrated?"

"Up and running on both the *Devil's Fortune* and the *Phoenix*. You will have a direct line of contact to us and vice versa."

"That's something, at least. You've heard what's happening?"

"I have. Most unfortunate, but at least the *Phoenix* was out of the hangar when they came."

"No small miracle, that," Twingo agreed. "I didn't want to do the final calibration and testing phase in the field, but we've made do with less before."

"Do you need any of us to accompany you?"

"I think we'll be good, but thanks. Doc, Crusher, and two others should be joining me shortly."

"Then, I will leave you to it. Good luck, Twingo. Ertz, I fear this may be goodbye for us."

"I will miss you, 755," Ertz said, looking near tears. "You and your brothers are welcome here any time."

"I will remember that," 755 said. "This was...peaceful. Thank you for your hospitality and friendship."

The battlesynth turned and walked back to the *Devil's Fortune*, which was now emitting a deep thrum as power was fed to the drives and the emitters charged. Twingo turned to Ertz and held out his hand.

"I suppose this will likely be goodbye for us as well. I believe Jason has been declared a fugitive and, until that can be changed, it just wouldn't be safe for you if we tried to come back. I'm going to miss you, my friend."

"I will miss all of you as well...except Kage. Tell Mr. Jason his businesses will be in good hands until he can return."

Twingo just smiled sadly and nodded. He'd seen things like this before and knew the unfortunate truth. They would never be returning to S'Tora. The place that had become their home and a place they truly loved no longer wanted them there, and that wouldn't change.

He turned and began the trudge over to where the *Phoenix* sat nearly a hundred meters away, parked on the hard-packed dirt. She looked magnificent, sleek, and dangerous. The ships most of the commercial yards were producing now were blocky, utilitarian affairs with no sense of artistry or aesthetic whatsoever. The DL-7 had gone through no fewer than four major overhauls since Jason had owned her, but now she was better than when she'd come out of the production facility at Jepsen Aero all those years ago.

About halfway to the ship, another ground car came rolling up.

This one was marked with the farm's logo, and he could see Doc driving. It came in fast and stopped abruptly. Doc was waving at him while two Galvetic warriors helped a third up into the ship while also carrying a few cases of equipment.

"We in a hurry?" Twingo asked, breaking into a jog.

"They're onto us," Doc said, passing him a transit crate and grabbing the last himself. "Not sure they tracked us here, but they showed up at the lab right as we were leaving. They already have Jason's house cordoned off and agents going through it."

"Damn. Not even a friendly letter asking us to kindly fuck off and leave," Twingo said. "You think we've been set up?"

"No idea, but we can talk about it once we're out of the S'Tora System."

Twingo took one last look at the rolling hills and bright sky and sighed heavily. S'Tora was a gem of a planet, and he was going to miss it.

7

"This is a terrible idea."

"Perhaps you just don't understand how brilliant it is," Jason said.

"No, I get it," Tauless said. "It's just bad. I can't believe you talked me into coming here for this."

"Would it help if I told you I missed you and that's why I asked?"

"No."

"These forgeries are passable but, without tying into the Kheprian database, they are not perfect," 701 said.

"I think we're good," Jason said. "They tie into the local system, and that will be as far as they check. They might flag them for additional query later when the slip-com traffic goes out but, by then, we'll be long gone. Like I said...this is a flawless plan."

Sepura Prime was a breathtaking planet. It was everything one expected from a Core World. The cities were clean and the buildings were beautiful examples of form and function in perfect balance.

It also had a highly evolved criminal underworld.

Jason called in some favors and was put in contact with a master forger who provided them credentials for Ayista Circ of Khepri.

Ayista was a special agent of the Kheprian Central Banking Authority's investigative branch. The fact that Ayista would be accompanied by an actual battlesynth would lend credence and fear to the presentation. All that had been missing was needing an actual pru, and the only one Jason knew well was Tauless, the poor engineer who had been put through the wringer during his association with Omega Force.

"How is Lucky doing?" Tauless asked.

"Other than being missing, he's great. The integration has been stable, and he's been back to his old self," Jason said.

"I'd like to see him again once this—whatever this all is—is over."

"Definitely," Jason said. "Come to S'Tora. We converted my beach house into a sweet party pad. It's great."

"I might do that."

"Are you two finished? It would probably be prudent to go over our mission details one more time before we attempt this," 701 said.

"There's a risk in over-prepping," Jason pointed out. 701 just stared at him for a moment.

"I think you are safe from that. We will go over it again until I am sure everyone understands their part."

For the next three hours, they refined and rehearsed their plan down to the last detail. They mapped out contingencies and possible escape routes should they be compromised. Jason was grudgingly forced to admit that perhaps 701 wasn't completely hapless when it came to this sort of covert operation. He seemed to be grasping that his biotic comrades couldn't take as much enemy weapons fire as he could. Like...none. That understanding was reflected in his risk management planning, working to give Tauless several abort and bugout options that would keep him alive if things went completely sideways.

"Keep in mind that the point here is to not have to shoot our way out," Jason said at one point.

"Correct," 701 confirmed. "But planning for all contingencies is still prudent."

"Fine," Jason sighed. "Let's go through it one more time."

"Can I help you and your...friend?"

"Let's hope so." Tauless handed over his forged credentials and stared at the attendant expectantly.

"Agent Circ, we were not expecting you or a visit from your agency at all." The credentials were handed back to Tauless without even being scanned.

"Announcing my visit would defeat the purpose, would it not?" he asked.

"And your companion?"

"Combat Unit 998," 701 said. "Kheprian Central Banking Authority Special Security Detachment."

"Of course. Please, excuse me while I get someone who might better assist you." The attendant practically ran from the lobby.

"So far, so good," Jason's voice came through over coms. Tauless said nothing.

"My apologies for the delay, Agent Circ!" A well-dressed *kidimin* came hurrying to them with that odd, bobbing gait beings with forward-bending knees had.

"It is of no consequence. I am here because of noted irregularities with one of your account holders. We are concerned as transfers were flagged in our office as having direct ties to known criminal enterprises. Given the seriousness of the enterprises in question, they sent us directly. I hope I can count on your cooperation Mr...."

"I'zan," the floor manager provided. "And I will, of course, assist anyone from the Central Banking Authority in any way I can."

"Excellent!" Tauless said. "Let's begin. The account holder in question belongs to a corporation called Omega Security Solutions based out of Niceen-3."

"That's in the Caspian Reaches?" I'zan asked. "I can see why that flagged. Let us go to a terminal, and we will start running traces. A moment if you please." He walked over to the attendant, speaking softly.

"701, can you amplify that and feed it back onto the com channel?" Jason asked.

"...checked his credentials?" I'zan was asking.

"Of course!" the attendant whispered. "It looked fine."

"Looked? You didn't run it through the computer?"

"Well, I... No. But he has a *battlesynth* with him. Who else would he be?"

"Great. Now, I will need to verify his identity somehow before he leaves here. Your incompetence will be noted."

"Is there an issue?" Tauless asked as I'zan walked back over.

"Just a small administrative task. If you would follow me, please."

Tauless and 701 were passed through a security checkpoint and led into the office area where I'zan waved them to a low-walled cubicle with a terminal. He sat at the terminal and waved them to the seats along the partition.

"The account information?"

Tauless handed over a datacard that had the information for the account that had just been opened under Jason's dummy corporation name. I'zan took it but hesitated.

"This terminal is behind the external security protocols," he said. "I-I shouldn't—"

"Mr. I'zan, the card has been sanitized. I brought it with me from our office, and it has never left my sight. Not only that, but I have never left the sight of Combat Unit 998. The chain of custody is intact, but you are absolutely in the right to verify that with me. Your diligence will be noted in my report."

"That is appreciated, sir." With the promise of reward, I'zan's paranoia evaporated, and he put the datacard onto the reader's surface without hesitation. "Beginning trace."

Tauless exchanged a look with 701 as I'zan began chasing the bogus Omega account all across the quadrant.

"Hopefully, we'll get what we came for," Tauless said.

I'zan nodded in agreement, unaware that the pru had just uttered a code phrase. Six seconds later, something slammed into the building with enough force to knock dust from the overhead light fixtures and send alarms blaring throughout the building. I'zan's head swiveled about just in time to see 701 spin around as if looking for a threat, catching him in the shoulder with his open hand with enough force to send him flying out of the cubicle.

"Mr. I'zan!" he exclaimed, moving to block the manager's view of his terminal. "My apologies. Are you injured?"

"I do not think I am injured, just stunned," I'zan said. "It was my fault for moving into your way, I'm sure. What was that?"

"The alarms have stopped," Tauless said, moving over beside 701. "Would you like me to summon medical help?"

"No," I'zan grunted. "No, thank you. I'm fine. Please, just help me up, and then we can continue."

"Your dedication to duty is admirable," Tauless said. "If you feel you are able—"

"Yes, of course." I'zan slid back into his seat and took a shuddering breath before continuing. "This account does indeed have many questionable transactions in and out, but nothing I can see as actionable. Whoever owns it is careful to keep things just below the threshold where our systems would issue an alert."

"Ours are a little more refined," Tauless said. "What is the current balance?"

"Less than a thousand credits. Just enough to keep it in the active category. Again, careful to not draw attention. How would you like to proceed?"

"There were no in-person transactions for this account?" Tauless asked, still playing the investigator.

"None. To be honest, this information could have been requested by your office remotely. We'd have been happy to send it."

"We've had false reports sent upon request as we've tried to track this down. Not this institution, of course, but it has happened more than once. We're afraid the owner of this account may have accomplices on the inside."

"Easy," Jason warned. "Don't give them too much reason to pursue this further."

"Not unheard of," I'zan said.

"Would it be possible for you to provide me with a list of transactions on this account?" Tauless said. "We will begin chasing threads from there, I suppose."

"At once." I'zan pulled a blank datacard from a container and placed it on the pad, uploading the transactional data. "There won't be much. This account isn't even a week old."

"I understand," Tauless said.

"I'm also afraid I must keep the datacard you brought in," I'zan said apologetically. "This is a firm rule for outside media. Now that it has accessed our secure system, it cannot leave through the security checkpoint until inspected and sanitized by our technicians. I have copied its contents onto the card I made for you."

"A sensible step," Tauless said. "Keep it."

"Might I also be so bold as to inspect your credentials?" I'zan said. "Protocol, I'm afraid."

"Come on," Jason's voice came over the com. "You guys are dragging this out too long. There's still a risk."

"Here you go," Tauless said, handing over the forged credentials and letting I'zan scan them. He tensed as the computer seemed to take an inordinately long amount of time.

"Ah, here we go. Everything is confirmed. Thank you for your patience, Agent Circ."

"While this was likely a dead end, we appreciate your cooperation, Mr. I'zan."

"Yes, of course. Now, if you'll both excuse me, I must escort you back through security so I can go and see what all the excitement was about earlier."

"What the hell is wrong with you two?" Jason demanded as Tauless and 701 climbed into the vehicle. "In and out. Not stand around for half an hour trading compliments like two dogs sniffing each other's asses!"

"Tauless performed well given that this is not his normal voca-tion," 701 said. "Your distraction was rather dramatic."

"I can only work with what I have. The local crews are a little hard to work with," Jason said. "I asked for something that would trigger an alarm. Instead, they drove a stolen commercial vehicle into the building and fled on foot. Did it work?"

"We had to improvise a bit, but we got the job done. When 701 knocked him to the floor, I put the card with the worm onto the pad. There should have been plenty of time for it to upload and embed itself into their system," Tauless said.

"Then, let's get the hell out of here," Jason said. "You want us to drop you anywhere?"

"I should be fine returning to Khepri aboard a starliner," Tauless said. "It would probably be best if we're not seen together." He pulled off the subtle modifications they'd made to his appearance to make sure he couldn't be identified from security recordings. He also wore a micro-dermal coating on all exposed skin surfaces to eliminate leaving any DNA or other damning evidence behind. Worked wonders, but itched like hell when it started peeling off.

"Suit yourself," Jason said. He programmed the vehicle to take them back to the hotel Tauless had been staying at. He'd drop the engineer off and, hopefully, be on the SX-5 and leaving the system within a few hours.

He was keenly aware of the time slipping by. So far, they'd been chasing shadows and no closer to finding Lucky and Kage than when they'd started, much less being able to craft a plan to rescue them.

"Patience, Captain," 701 said as if reading his thoughts. "Lucky will know to drag this out as long as possible to give you the time you need."

8

"He is waiting for you inside."

"I assumed as much," Lucky said. "You were not asked to join us?"

"Just watch yourself," Suta said.

Lucky held the glare for a moment before walking through the hatch and into a luxuriously appointed lounge. Ancula sat on a sofa, drink in hand. When he saw the battlesynth, he actually smiled.

"Thank you for joining me, Lucky."

"Thank you for pretending I had a choice."

"We always have choices, my friend. It's just the consequences we don't like."

"True."

"Family is everything, don't you think?" Ancula asked, standing up to pace the room. Lucky's sensors were picking up enough evaporated alcohol in the air to know that the Vissalo had been in drinking for some time before he called for him.

"There are many types of family," Lucky answered.

"Precisely!" Ancula said. "You understand that! You have your family that you adopted. They trust you, and you try to protect them.

It's what made you take such a high degree of risk for your Veran friend. It's why you don't kill Suta and attempt to take control of my ship. You sacrifice your own wellbeing for your family."

"I would also kill for them," Lucky said.

"As I would for mine," Ancula said, his voice a low growl. "I will admit that I've developed a certain fondness for your bluntness and honesty during our time together. When I found out the mimic function of your body had been removed, I was torn as to what I should do next. While that unique feature would have made my task much simpler, I have come to understand you are still a unique creature with talents I may still be able to exploit to achieve my goal."

"And what is your goal, Ancula?"

"Family, Lucky. Family," Ancula whispered. "I want mine back."

Things took shape in Lucky's mind and Ancula's somewhat erratic behavior started to make sense. This wasn't just some heist. This was deeply personal. Lucky knew a little about the typical Vissalo family structure. They evolved to encourage genetic diversity by the females choosing multiple partners over their reproductive years while males, who only bred once or twice in a lifetime, would remain with the young and raise them. The family unit was usually the male and the children, while the females often had no contact afterwards and formed their own small, cloistered groups together.

Given Ancula's probable age, Lucky assumed that by *family*, he was referring to offspring from a second, midlife breeding. Vissalo males didn't tend to stay attached to their offspring once they were old enough to leave on their own, but that wasn't a firm rule.

"Your family was taken?" Lucky asked.

"Indeed," Ancula said, regaining his composure. "Taken by my enemies, but with the aid of a corrupt government. That is our task, my reluctant friend. We must find a way to safely secure their release. Before you ask, yes...I have exhausted all diplomatic options available to me. Even as extensive as my network is, the people holding them are beyond my reach."

"You seek a military solution?"

"It wasn't my first choice. I had wanted you to simply walk in and take them by pretending to be someone with the power to do so. Now we must adjust our plan."

"We? I am to be involved in these planning stages?"

"We will speak further." Ancula waved toward the hatch in an obvious dismissal. "The situation is delicate, and we will need to be precise. Go see your friend. We will speak of details later."

Lucky walked back out of the lounge and was immediately accosted by Suta.

"What did he want with you?" the deranged synth demanded.

"That is between him and I," Lucky said. "If you wish to know, ask him yourself."

"You think I cannot see what is happening?" Suta said, stepping in closer.

"One more step, and I will assume you are a threat," Lucky said, turning to face him.

"And?"

"I will neutralize the threat. Step aside. Now."

The standoff went on for several tense seconds before Suta flinched and took a step back.

"I'll be watching you."

Lucky said nothing as he walked off, showing his back to his enemy in an overt sign of contempt. He hadn't considered that Suta would become jealous as Lucky was drawn further into Ancula's confidence. The Vissalo was surrounded by conscripts with nobody to confide in, and while Suta served a purpose, the psychopathic synth wasn't much of a conversationalist or filled with any sort of empathy. Now, he seemed to summon Lucky with regularity to his private areas aboard the ship to simply talk while Suta stood outside, uninvited and unwelcome. It was an interesting new dynamic Lucky thought could be turned to his advantage.

So far, the ship had made port four different times, but Lucky was not privy to what they were taking on or dropping off, nor would Ancula tell him. He had no idea if they were part of the upcoming operation or not. The lack of information made him reluctant to risk sending out a coded transmission to one of Omega

Force's dead drops. Slip-com nodes couldn't be jammed, but they could be detected. He had no doubt that if he tried to send word to the captain, Ancula would know immediately. Far better to keep that capability a secret until he could actually use it to his advantage.

He continued down and aft in the ship until he made his way to the infirmary, nodding to the staff and walking through as they were now used to seeing him multiple times a day. When he walked into Kage's room, the Veran was lying back, eyes closed, and pretending to be asleep. He walked over and slid a hand under Kage's left palm. The gesture would look like nothing more than simple affection to anyone looking in.

"How did it go?" Kage's voice broadcast in Lucky's head through the inductive link they created by Kage's nanite chains latching onto Lucky's skin.

"This is a recovery mission. Rescue, to be more accurate. Ancula has family that is being held captive, and he needed Seven to impersonate an official to get them out," Lucky sent back.

"Interesting. Perhaps I can work with that. I'm close to getting access to a Nexus link the next time this ship makes orbit someplace. How are things going with your old buddy?"

"I have not killed him yet, but I have come close. There is an interesting new dynamic, and I think I can drive a wedge between him and Ancula. The more I can make Suta seem erratic and unstable, the easier it will be for me to convince Ancula he is a liability."

"What do you need from me?"

"Try and find me a destination, or even just a current location. If I do not know where we are, I cannot send word to the others and give them a general search area."

"Be careful. This ship has sophisticated internal sensors to track all the unwilling guests and their activities. Your slip-com transmitter will be detected as soon as the field generator comes online."

"Noted. Is there anything you need?"

"I'm solid. The staff here isn't stupid. They know I'm faking, but they aren't saying anything about it to Ancula's command staff. I

bank into their system given all that. They're a little fussy when it comes to unsanctioned military action."

"Not as much as you might think," 701 said. "The Kheprian people might be squeamish, but the government has no such qualms. When they cannot be seen sending their regular military, they will hire contractors."

"Hence why they have their banking network extend to a planet full of military contractors." Jason nodded.

"Ancula is preparing to hire a mercenary force," 701 said.

"Ancula is a criminal. If he needed shooters he could pull from his own ranks or hire known mercs through his contacts," Jason said, considering the problem. "He needs cannon fodder, and he needs it to be anonymous. He's hiding something from his organization, and he's shuffling money around to buy himself a secret army."

"Plausible," 701 admitted. "Likely, even," he said more grudgingly. "How do we find what the target might be?"

"There's the million-credit question," Jason said. "Whatever it is, it's almost certain to be why he's captured Lucky and Kage."

"What do you want to do next?"

"Let's reposition to Enzola-2. He's sent all his money there. Maybe he'll show up to spend it."

"This isn't too bad," Jason said after letting the local starport customs officer inspect the SX-5. The bribe to look the other way about the ship's weaponry and questionable logs wasn't even that exorbitant.

"Like Niceen-3 in the Caspian Reaches," 701 said. "The consortium that runs Enzola-2 understands that a planet dangerous to the causal traveler is a planet that cannot attract investors, only the attention of more powerful predators like the ConFed."

"Whatever it is, it works for me if it means I can sleep in a hotel without getting shivved in the middle of the night or kept up from gunfights in the streets," Jason said.

"Do you have a plan here that does not involve impersonating a Kheprian official?"

"I like to play it by ear." Jason shrugged. "Something always pops up."

"Burke! You no good son of a bitch!" a voice bellowed across the tarmac.

"See?" Jason said. "Trust the process."

An angry *dracle* stormed across the tarmac at them, his head plumage standing straight up like a mohawk and quivering.

"He looks quite angry," 701 remarked.

"I always hoped I would run into you again," the dracle said.

"I was sort of hoping the opposite," Jason said. "Still pissed about that little incident way back when, Arddle?"

"I lost my protection license on Eshquaria thanks to you fools!" Arddle spluttered.

"To be fair, that was mostly Crusher." Jason shrugged. "And it's not like you didn't have it coming. You cheated us out of a contract by bribing an official to impound my ship. We were just returning the favor."

"By implicating me in a political assassination?! It took me a year to clear my name. I lost everything!"

"Let's just agree to disagree," Jason said. "You screwed me out of a contract, Crusher almost had you imprisoned for the rest of your life. I think we can all learn a lesson here about—"

"Shut your mouth!" Arddle screamed. Their conflict was now gaining the attention of others including the uniformed starport security.

"Whatever happens next, don't react," Jason whispered into his hand before stepping away from 701 and closer to Arddle. "I'm not sure what you're complaining about. Eshquarian prisons are like a resort. To be honest, you should be thanking me."

What little restraint that had been holding Arddle back let go. He lashed out with an open hand strike, telegraphing the hit with the way his shoulder rolled. Jason let it connect, spinning on the ball of his left foot with the hit to lessen the blow but still make it look real.

He fell to the tarmac and rolled to his back just as Arddle, predictable as ever, pulled a sidearm and aimed it at him.

Jason shook his head at 701 as the battlesynth raised his hand, no doubt about to switch to combat mode and neutralize the threat. What Arddle's rage-clouded brain hadn't registered yet was the trio of Port Authority troopers sprinting across the tarmac toward them, pulling their weapons.

"Please!" he wailed. "Don't let him kill me!"

"Lower the weapon! Now!" a trooper shouted. Arddle looked about in confusion.

"Me?!" he screamed. "I am the aggrieved! By my right of—" That was all he got out as two of the troopers fired heavy stunners. Arddle dropped in a heap, twitching sporadically as the stunner shots overloaded his nervous system.

"Are you injured, sir?" the lead trooper asked.

"Not badly," Jason said, making some show of standing up on shaky legs. "But only because you showed up so quickly. I can't thank you enough."

"Do you know your assailant?"

"Never seen him before. He started screaming about how some human had ripped him off, and then took a swing at me."

"I will need to see your ident," the trooper said. "We'll detain him and open an investigation, but he'll not be bothering you during your stay here."

Jason handed over a standard ConFed ident passport that had him listed as Buck Rogers from Pinnacle Station. The trooper scanned it, and then, once his computer showed no outstanding warrants or fines, handed it back over without a word. They collected Arddle's still-twitching body and moved away a bit to make room for the vehicle coming toward them for pickup.

"I suppose there was some point to all that other than your own amusement?" 701 asked.

"Arddle is a guildmaster in one of the larger merc brokerages in the Upper Cygnus region. Makes sense he's here if they're running entire PMCs off this world," Jason said.

"That did not answer my question."

"He'll have access to the contract boards before a private operator like me."

"And?"

"If Ancula is coming with a pile of money to hire a team of specialized operators, he'll have to do it through the guilds. Brokers will go to pitch to the guys like Arddle to begin recruiting. We just need to get to his files, and we can hopefully find out what sort of specialists Ancula is after."

"How will you access his files?" 701 asked.

"His ship is right over there," Jason pointed across the tarmac. "And he helpfully forgot to close the boarding hatch before coming over and assaulting me."

"You *planned* this?" 701 was incredulous.

"Of course not," Jason scoffed. "But like I said...things just sort of work out."

They went to Arddle's ship, an expensive high-speed courier model from Euchan, one of the more exclusive small ship builders on Aracoria. Jason looked it over appreciatively. Apparently, just being the middleman without getting involved too much in the actual shooting paid pretty damn well.

"It would be more efficient to download his entire com buffer and parse it aboard the SX-5," 701 said. "It might be prudent to relocate to a different starport sooner than later."

"Good idea," Jason said, pulling a beat-up slicer module Kage and Twingo had developed together and went forward in the ship to where he assumed the com room would be.

The com terminals were all locked out, but the module still made quick work of it. Jason set it near a data port and activated the device, watching as nanite tendrils flowed into the port to establish a connection. He looked around the ship, resisting the urge to vandalize it. They needed to leave without a trace.

"This Arddle seemed to have a notably elevated level of hatred toward you," 701 remarked from the ship's luxurious common area.

"I won't say it's completely undeserved," Jason said. "This was years ago when we were barely getting by. He had a crew that was competing for a cushy, high-paying protection gig with us, so he used his contacts to have the *Phoenix* inspected by the locals and ultimately impounded. The money we had to pay to get the ship released and clear our names with the Eshquarian authorities damn near bankrupted us.

"To return the favor, Crusher tracked down one of the VIPs Arddle had a crew protecting and mugged them."

"Lord Felex, the Guardian Archon of Galvetor, assaulted an innocent civilian in the streets to prove a point?" 701 asked.

"You make it sound worse than it was. He didn't permanently harm them," Jason said. "Then, he did it to two more clients, making sure he said cryptic shit about Arddle each time. Word got out that someone was targeting his clients over a personal grudge, and Eshquaria yanked his protection license. At the time, that was his main source of income. Apparently, he's been angry about that ever since."

"Apparently."

"Either way, he seems to be doing okay now. This ship isn't cheap, and he's come a long way from babysitting VIPs. Now, he's recruiting armies to let warlords and crime bosses inflict untold horrors on some innocent populus for fun and profit."

"You are quite cynical about a profession you have been a part of for many years," 701 pointed out.

"We try to be a little more selective," Jason said. "We could make more money taking any contract that comes along, but we prefer to hit the people who have it coming. Especially Lucky. He's always been adamant about no harm to innocents."

"I would expect no less. His moral code is inflexible. It is one of the—" 701's head snapped around. "Someone approaches."

Jason walked back and saw two more dracle walking directly toward the ship wearing the same blue jackets Arddle had been in.

"Shit," he muttered, running back to the com room and checking on the device. "I need another minute or so."

"I will handle it," 701 said and walked out. "I will meet you back at our ship."

"Hang on," Jason said. "What the hell are you about to do?"

He was talking to himself. 701 was already out of the ship.

"Son of a bitch!"

10

"Stop him!"

701 broke into a sprint away from the ship, a small package clutched tightly to his chest.

"Stop!"

701 had no idea what he'd taken. He had simply ripped a conveniently sized transit case from out of the cargo netting and took off at a run from the approaching dracle. As he'd hoped, they'd pursued, assuming he had stolen something of value. He let them close just enough to keep them interested until he was out of sight of Arddle's ship, then he accelerated toward a squat service building. As he neared the building, he fired his repulsors, arcing high over the building but bobbling the case and dropping it.

The case fell onto the roof of the building as he'd hoped, and he continued on his trajectory, landing on the other side hard enough to crack the tarmac. He ran straight to a line of parked service vehicles and disappeared into them as the two dracle came puffing around the corner of the building.

"What the hell was that thing?" one asked.

"No idea. I didn't get a good look, and it had some sort of protective suit on," the other wheezed. "It dropped case on top of the building. We need to get it back down before Arddle gets back."

"Where is he anyway?"

"Who cares? Let's just button the ship back up so we don't get our pay docked again."

701 watched from between two refuelers as the pair walked around the building, trying to figure out a way up onto the roof. Thankfully, the pair wasn't overly bright and couldn't identify him nor did they seem inclined to report the incident to their boss. If he could avoid being spotted on his way back to the SX-5, they would have gotten away clean.

As he snuck his way through the vehicles, trying to avoid both the dracle and starport personnel, he reflected on the day's completely unlikely chain of events. Jason Burke truly appeared to operate on a not insignificant trust that his own luck would turn up something. 701 had observed the human for some time, wondering what it was about the creature's leadership that would make 777 pledge such undying loyalty. Burke's strategic and tactical thinking left much to be desired yet, more often than not, he was able to affect a favorable outcome. Could there be some intangible, undetectable power that humans possessed that allowed them to intuit situations that logical thinking could not? Was Burke a special case among his people?

These were the things he pondered in the quiet hours as the human slept. In addition to Burke himself, his son, Jacob Brown, had somehow lured away their leader. 707, now absurdly allowing himself to be called Tin Man, had left the unit to live and work among humans. What was it about these strange little aliens that enchanted his lot mates so? And not just the battlesynths. The Guardian Archon of Galvetor had abandoned his people, abandoned his title, just to follow Burke around getting in scraps on backwater worlds nobody cared about for causes nobody would ever remember.

It was a problem he intended to research further during his time with Jason Burke. Perhaps there was an obvious answer he was missing in how to best bring his lot mates home.

Jason sat on the SX-5, watching the two dracle goons make some show of securing their ship while the computer chewed through the data he'd pulled from Arddle's com system. So far, it was promising. Since he knew how much money Ancula had and where it would be, it helped him create a search algorithm to dig through the thousands of open contracts and pick out the most likely one that would lead them to Lucky and Kage.

One variable he hadn't counted on was that the funds Ancula had transferred were likely for the entire expedition not just manpower. That widened the search more than he would have liked.

"Progress?" 701 asked as he climbed up the ramp.

"Some," Jason said. "More than I'd hoped, actually. Arddle isn't trying to fill any of the contracts that might be for Ancula, but he's got all the information on them."

"Suggested course of action?" 701 asked.

"There are five, maybe seven contracts that look promising if our theory about why Ancula is hiding and shuffling money is current," Jason said. "Those are being serviced by a brokerage in a city called... Kavena. It's a nine-hour flight unless we head back up to orbit."

"I think staying in the atmosphere will gain us less attention," 701 said.

"Agreed. I'm calling for clearance now. They won't hold Arddle too much longer. They'll rough him up, extort him for money, and then send him on his way."

"What is our plan? And please do not say that *something will turn up.*"

"You'll love this one."

"I will not."

"We're going to get ourselves hired onto Ancula's merc crew."

"I stand corrected. I actually *do* like this one."

"Enzola-2. What do you think?"

"I have been here before," Lucky said.

"I'm sure," Ancula said. "I'm also sure you know why we're here."

"You're going to hire more military assets for the recovery operation. This would certainly be the place to do it. Entire military companies are on the surface for hire."

"That they are. It's fortunate I have such a knowledgeable mercenary such as you available to help with the process, don't you think?"

"I would assume you would be just as knowledgeable given your line of work," Lucky said.

"My line of work has nothing to do with violence or death," Ancula said with some heat. "That is a Vissalo stereotype I do not appreciate."

"You are a criminal, are you not?" Lucky pushed. "Are not most of the crew on this ship here under some form of coercion?"

"I am a facilitator," Ancula said. "I hide money and assets from governments for some very bad people. I also peddle in information and access. I have hooks into hundreds of planetary governments, usually through blackmail, that I am able to exploit. I suppose your point is well taken and, yes, many of the crew here weren't willing volunteers.

"But they will be generously compensated once their debt to me is paid. As will you. Help me recover my family, and I will make you wealthy."

"Money means little to me," Lucky said. "All I ask is that Kage be allowed to leave with me unharmed."

"I stand by my word," Ancula said. "He will not be harmed, and you will both be free to leave when your task is complete."

"My task being?"

"At the moment? You will take a shuttle to the surface and supervise filling key positions from the contractors down there," Ancula was once again all business. "I have a brokerage that is assembling potential candidates. Once you have selected them, I will give the final approval, and then I will send another ship down to collect them."

"You do not want them aboard this one?"

"Not at all. These are dangerous, unpredictable people. The ship we have to transport them to the staging area is specially equipped to deal with them. Once there, you will begin to train them for the mission."

"I am surprised you are having me do this and not Suta," Lucky said.

"Suta..." Ancula turned and began pacing the lounge. "He is... complicated. Tell me, does your kind suffer from mental instability as you age?"

"It is inevitable," Lucky said. "Depending on the primary matrix type code, it can set in earlier than others. Has something happened?"

"No," Ancula waved him off. "Well, not recently. I've just noticed in recent years that his propensity for violence has become much more defined. And indiscriminate."

"I see."

"Not your concern. What my point was is that Suta, while trusted completely by me, would err on the side of picking the most violent, destructive contractors available. This mission will require a more precise sort of operator."

"I understand," Lucky said.

"Good. The parameters for the personnel needed are here." Ancula handed him a datacard. "Study them, and then I want you on the shuttle to the surface within the next two hours." As Lucky turned to leave, he held up his hand.

"Go back down to engineering and have that pack removed. I don't want to risk it triggering when you leave the ship. At this point, I don't think it is needed anymore."

"We have assembled top notch talent for your consideration... Ah, I didn't get your name, sir."

"I did not give it to you," Lucky said, reading over the list of candidates and selecting the ones he thought were a match to move on to the second round of elimination.

"I... Of course, sir."

"I am not being deliberately rude or pointlessly mysterious," Lucky assured the brokerage representative. "But my employer insists upon his privacy, and that extends to those that work for him. You may call me Seven."

Seven had never operated on Enzola-2, preferring instead to stick to the frontier regions, so Lucky felt comfortable using it as an alias.

"Very good, sir. You have made your selections?"

"Yes. Please, have these candidates brought to the evaluation center at once," Lucky handed the tablet back to the rep.

"It will be done."

The rep scurried out of the reception lounge, and Lucky rose from the chair, still not comfortable sitting on furniture despite his new form being small and light compared to his old one. Ancula had sent him down alone to handle the selection process, something that had shocked him. Once he made his final selections, and Ancula cleared them, the transport would come down and payment would be transferred. The mercs he was hiring on Enzola-2 would never meet Ancula or step foot on his ship.

Lucky took note of the special care his captor was taking in staying isolated from the operation. He knew that odds were high Ancula would try to have him and Kage killed as they were loose ends that knew far too much. He would need to find a way to convince Ancula that Kage was vital to the operation and get him off the ship where he could control the situation better. The Vissalo might take exception to being a brutal killer because he hides behind the sophistry of hiring it out to contractors, but Lucky saw how ruthless and calculating he was.

11

"Master Seven, your prospective contractors have been gathered."

Lucky stepped from the open-air vehicle and approached where a group of nearly one hundred and fifty mercs and specialists milled about. From this group, he would pick the sixty-two needed for Ancula's rescue mission. There were the usual species represented like Taukkir, Korkaran, and Eshquarian. The one that stood out immediately was a battlesynth near the back of the group, staring at him intently.

Though his species looked identical to most, Lucky was able to recognize 701. Once he spotted his old lot mate, he saw that the figure next to him wearing a combat helmet had a stature identical to that of Jason Burke. He had no idea how they'd found him, but now he had two more people to worry about. It was also curious that they had paired up given their mutual disdain for each other.

"We will begin immediately," Lucky announced loudly. "Divide up into your respective skill groups and await further instruction."

As he would have expected, the bulk of the group were soldier-class, with smaller groups breaking into the various specialty skill classes that Ancula had requested. Those had been pre-screened already, and he knew who would be accompanying the others to the transport. His main task on the surface was to lay eyes on the soldiers and make certain they were who and what they said they were. The appearance of two of his friends just complicated that. He had to figure out what they were planning and if he should even allow them to continue on.

"Guild ident," he said, holding his hand out once he was standing in front of Jason. The captain handed it over without a word. Lucky touched it to the handheld scanner he carried and looked over the forged credentials his friend was using.

"There a problem?" Jason asked, his modulated voice harsh.

"David Byrne of Niceen-3," Lucky read, ignoring him. "Expert in small unit combat, ship-to-ship operations, and veteran of three major campaigns within the Concordian Cluster during the ConFed occupation."

"And?"

"You are asking for twice the standard guild rates for your experience rating," Lucky said.

"I'm worth it," Jason countered.

"That is not what this says," Lucky held up the scanner. "You will get standard rates or you will not be coming at all."

"This is bullshit," Jason grabbed his ident from Lucky. "You clowns are recruiting for a job that needs a lot of shooters, and you don't provide any threat brief. You're lucky I showed up at all. I get double or I walk, and I promise you'll wish I was there judging by some of the scrubs I see in this hall."

Lucky stared at him for a moment, resisting the urge to punch him in the head.

"One-point-five, not double," Lucky said. "Are you in or out?"

"Guess that's the best deal I'm getting," Jason grumbled. "I'm in."

"Over there with the others," Lucky pointed before moving on and stepping in front of 701. "Deserter?"

"No," 701 said.

"Battlesynths are too memorable, and chances are good it will bring down the wrath of the Kheprian government on us. Why should my employer take a risk like that?"

"Because I will work for standard rates, and I am worth more than twenty of the other fighters you have here, including the loudmouth fool you just spoke to."

"Go with the others."

Lucky made some show of reviewing the others, even though he had already determined who he would be taking. Letting Jason and 701 into the mix meant he had to omit two of his previous choices, but there was no doubt they would be able to integrate into the group. After completing his review, he waved over Ancula's finance administrator and gave him the list.

"All of these," he said. "This puts us well within the personnel budget, and I was pleasantly surprised at the quality available here."

"Got it," the administrator said.

"Do you need my assistance setting up payment with the guild-masters for anonymity?"

"Don't concern yourself with that. Just do your job."

Lucky watched him walk away, suspicion gnawing at him. For someone whose job was to protect his boss's financial interests, he didn't seem particularly interested in the numbers.

"Everyone has passed inspection," another of Ancula's people said to him. "The second transport is on the way down to collect them. Once they're aboard, the boss wants you back on the shuttle."

"I will not be staying with this team?"

"Boss said he wants you back on his ship, so that's where you're going."

"Understood."

Lucky gave his friends one last look before leaving out the doors he came in through. Whatever plan Jason had cooked up appeared to be more subtle than just coming in guns blazing. Even though Lucky didn't like the fact two more of his friends were in danger, there was some comfort to be had in that he had assets close at hand Ancula wasn't aware of.

The walk to the waiting shuttle gave him some time to think about how best to employ this new advantage. For now, he would wait. Once the mission started, there would be confusion and cover. That would be their best chance to break free and escape, but only if he could free Kage from Ancula's grasp first. To do that, he would need to continue playing the confidant and gain a level of trust he did not quite have yet.

"That went well," 701 said quietly. "I assumed we would be split up."

Jason just grunted in reply, certain that the transport they were on was loaded with audio and video sensors to observe them no matter where they went.

"Still no word what this job is yet," he said. "Hopefully, there will be at least a summary brief and a chance to walk if they're about to send us into a meat grinder."

"I'm not sure I understand."

Jason just sighed. The battlesynth was still quite hopeless when it came to covert work.

"That a real battlesynth?" a harsh voice said. Jason and 701 turned to look at the newcomer. "Or just some knockoff?"

"I have no idea who you are, and I don't care," Jason said as two more joined the first. They were bipeds, heavily muscled, with a blue-green hue to their skin. It was impossible to determine exactly what they might be since those characteristics were shared by so many species in the quadrant. "Get lost."

"I'm just asking a question," the leader said as the other two spread out a bit to flank them. "After all, I think I deserve to know who it is that bumped our two brothers off this job. Don't you think so?"

"What I think is that you're about to bite off a hell of a lot more than you can chew," Jason said. "Just walk away."

"Oh, we'll be walking away. Don't worry about that."

In what was tediously predictable, the two flankers rushed in from the sides. As soon as Jason detected the movement, he did what was least expected; he launched himself toward the leader. The alien was taken off guard by the human's speed and reflexes, and Jason slammed into him before he could even raise his arms in defense. Once on the ground, Jason slammed his helmet into the face of his opponent with enough force to shatter bone. That single hit was all it took to end the fight.

701, as Jason had expected, took care of business with little effort. After Jason climbed to his feet to check on his companion, it appeared that the battlesynth had simply grabbed one of the aliens and used him as a club to beat the third almost to death.

"Nice," he said. A moment later, alarms began blaring, and armed troopers ran into the hold.

"Nobody moves, nobody dies," a bored sounding voice said from the now-open hatch. "It never fails. Whenever we're contracted to transport a group of you killers for hire, you have to make a mess of my ship for the first bit.

"Let me take this opportunity to set the rules since the festivities seem to have begun early. My crew has guns. Lots of them. You all do not. If you can't behave on my ship, you will be tossed off, and it matters little to me where the ship is when that happens. I hear being ejected from a vessel in slip-space is especially painful for the fraction of a second you live through it."

"How would you know?" Jason asked.

"Excuse me?" the captain asked. Guns drifted in Jason's direction.

"How would you know it's painful? I can't imagine someone survived to come back and tell how it felt."

The captain nodded at one of his troopers who, without hesitation, raised their weapon and shot Jason right in the chest with a high-power stunner. The soft armor he wore absorbed some of the energy, but Jason was still sent to the deck writhing in pain. The trooper looked on in surprise that he wasn't knocked out completely and raised his weapon again, but the captain stopped him.

"Hold," he said, walking over to where the human lay on the deck gasping. He looked up at 701. "I'm not going to have any trouble out of you for zapping your partner, am I?"

"I cannot properly express how entertaining I found that," 701 said. "Thank you." The captain looked at him in confusion before crouching next to Jason.

"Did you understand this object lesson about how I expect you to conduct yourself aboard my ship?"

"I don't even remember my name after that asshole shot me," Jason groaned, earning some laughter from the onlookers.

"I have a feeling we are going to have trouble with you," the captain said, standing up. He waved at his troopers again and pointed to the three badly injured aliens on the deck. "Have them collected and sent to the infirmary. The contract states they need to arrive more or less intact."

Jason climbed to his feet while more crewmembers came in to take the injured parties to get fixed up. The crowd dispersed, and the captain came in close to Jason and motioned for him to remove the helmet.

"What was that really all about?" he asked once Jason had pulled it off.

"My partner and I were last minute additions to this job. Apparently, there were five of them, and we bumped two of their friends."

"They won't drop this just because you beat them this once. Better watch your back."

"Unfortunately, you're probably right," Jason said. "I don't think they'll try it again aboard your ship, but once we get to our destination, I'm expecting an ambush or two."

"Tough business. Try not to cause me any more problems while you're aboard."

"Interesting interaction," 701 said once the captain and his troopers left.

"I'm sure he was about to try and sell me a protection package," Jason said. "If I asked him to protect me from those three, he'd ask for half my share on this job for a private cabin. Then, he'd go to them and offer them another crack at me for a price. He'd then hedge either way."

"This seems to be a profession that attracts those without honor or codes of conduct."

"You have no idea."

12

"Did you make him *stronger* than he was before?"

"Eh, not by too much. Just returned him back to where he was at his peak." Doc watched his monitors as Crusher entered the obstacle course for the fifth time and showed no signs of slowing. "I appreciate the use of the facilities."

"We really don't use these training grounds anymore," UAES Marine Captain Jacob Brown said. "Newer facilities were built on the other side of the base. So, why are Mazer and Morakar here with you guys?"

"It's complicated," Doc said. "To be brief, Crusher talked me into doing this sort of genetic tweak without explaining to me that it was a taboo punishable by excommunication or death on his world. During the process of building the serum package, I discovered a deep, dark state secret. The brothers are here to try and make sure the Galvetic Empire doesn't catch wind of what I did."

"How will they do this?" Tin Man asked. The battlesynth had accompanied Jacob but had said very little.

"No idea," Doc said. "All I know is that they probably won't kill him."

"Any word from my dad?"

"Not yet. He disappeared with 701 to go after Lucky and Kage. It's been quiet since they left. Twingo was able to remotely connect to the SX-5, and she's parked on a planet called Enzola-2 right now with zero damage or alerts. Whatever they're up to, the ship is in good shape at least."

"What is the status of the *Phoenix*?" Tin Man asked.

"You'd have to ask Twingo," Doc said. "We made it out here in one piece, but he didn't seem to be all that happy with how she performed."

"I wish I could take some leave and head out with you guys but, right now, things are tense around here. Earth just left the Cridal Cooperative, and the political situation is volatile," Jacob said.

"Things are bad all over right now," Doc said. "The majority of minor powers are waking up to the reality of the ConFed actually being gone and Miressa Prime no longer sending out fleets to squash regional skirmishes. It's going to be a long season of the strong preying on the weak I fear."

"That felt good," Crusher said as he jogged up to where they stood. He was covered in sweat but, otherwise, you couldn't tell he'd been going through a grueling course for nearly forty minutes.

"Your levels all looked good," Doc said. "Much better than when we started. How do you feel right now? No uncontrollable urges to kill anyone standing here?"

"Only you, but I can control it."

"Another improvement," Doc muttered as he made notes.

"What's the idea of your father sneaking off again without us?" Crusher demanded, leveling a finger at Jacob.

"He doesn't tell me shit." Jacob shrugged. "He mentioned Lucky was missing when I last talked to him, and then, the next thing I know, you guys come here saying you got his house confiscated and needed a place to crash."

"Likely story," Crusher said before turning back to Doc. "So? Am I done?"

"Done?" Doc asked. "No, you're not done. But you are stable both physically and mentally. I know you don't appreciate how difficult this was, but you're actually quite lucky I was able to correct the issues at all."

"I was under the impression the Archive assisted you," Tin Man said.

"What's your point?" Doc snapped.

"Only that the most advanced AI in known space might have made your difficult task some small measure easier than you are making it out to be."

"He has a point," Crusher said.

"I can still let the Reddix brothers have you," Doc said. "They were quite happy to handle—" His words were drowned out by an ear-shattering roar as the *Phoenix* tore over the remote area, her downwash ripping up vegetation and almost taking them off their feet. The gunship pulled up into a steep climb, engines still thundering, and was quickly out of sight.

"I guess the low-level flight mode glitches have been worked out," Jacob said.

Ten minutes later, the *Phoenix* came in again, much slower and with her gear down. She touched down softly on the hardpacked dirt beside the training complex building they'd been using as a temporary base of operations with the blessing of the base commander, Admiral Marcus Webb. Jacob Brown and members of his scout team had come out to meet them and offer what limited assistance they were authorized. Scout Fleet was still part of Earth's military, and Webb didn't want his people tied in too closely to whatever illegal escapades the Omega Force crew might be up to.

"Damn this thing is badass!" Navy Commander Ryan "Sully" Sullivan said as he walked down off the ramp. "Can we get one?"

Sully was the pilot of Jacob's team and had volunteered to help Twingo give the ship a more rigorous shakedown than the engineer was capable of. Since Jacob had stolen the *Phoenix* once before, Sully had a lot of seat time flying her and had always had a soft spot for the gunship.

"That thing is older than we are put together," Jacob said. "They're not building gunships like that anymore."

"Not exactly," Twingo said. "The new Jepsen Aero has a new line coming out that is similar to the old DL-series. Talk to your boss and make him buy you one."

"Yeah, right," Jacob said.

They milled about in the cool early evening air until the Reddix brothers pulled back up in their borrowed vehicle. As representatives of the Galvetic Legions, they'd asked for an unofficial meeting with Admiral Webb to discuss some of the political shakeups in the quadrant. Doc couldn't be sure, but it seemed to him that they were interested in opening lines of communication with an eye toward recommending to Galvetor that they approach Earth about a mutual defense pact. The Empire had a mighty infantry but hardly any fleet to speak of. That was an untenable position in a galaxy where wars were won and lost in space. It would be interesting to see what a Galvetor-Earth alliance might look like, especially one that was initiated by the warrior class.

"We are ready to leave whenever you are," Mazer said. Like Morakar, Mazer had pointedly ignored Crusher the entire flight. To say it had been awkward would be putting it mildly.

"I suppose Enzola-2 is our most logical step. If nothing else, we can check on the SX-5 and try and track their movements from there," Doc said. "Captain Brown, thank you for your assistance. I'll let your father know how you are when I catch up to him."

"It was good seeing you guys again," Jacob said, embracing Doc, and then Twingo. "All of you." He paused at Crusher, unsure what to do, but the big warrior grabbed him and wrapped him up in an enormous hug, lifting him off the ground.

"Now that you work in space and we're homeless again, maybe we'll run into each other more often," Twingo said.

After more prolonged goodbyes, they boarded the *Phoenix*. Doc climbed into the pilot's seat and checked the instruments before engaging the drive and lifting them smoothly from the ground.

"Better," he said approvingly. "That surging is gone."

"It's still there," Twingo said, frowning. "But we've dampened it enough you won't feel it under most circumstances. The good news is that the self-calibration subsystem is now fully integrated and functioning properly. The longer we fly her, the smoother the ride will become."

"Setting course for Enzola-2," Doc said. "That is... Damn, that's a long flight time. Why couldn't the captain pull this stunt on this side of the quadrant?"

"Where did our Galvetic buddies go?" Twingo asked.

"They never came up on the bridge. There's been a bit of tension between them since the brothers showed up," Doc said.

"That's one way to put it." Twingo snorted. "I'm just trying to stay out of the way so I don't get caught up in any crossfire."

"You will speak to me. Now!"

Mazer turned his head slowly to gaze up at the warrior who had once been Felex Tezakar. He stood on the small mezzanine that led onto the main deck while Mazer and his brother had taken up residence in the cargo hold.

"We do not speak to traitors," he said.

"You dare call me a traitor?!" Crusher bellowed, leaping off the mezzanine and slamming into the deck with a hard *thud*. His nostrils flared in rage, and his eyes were red-rimmed. "After all I have done for you?!"

"You have betrayed your oath, betrayed our trust, and you did it because, underneath the title of Guardian Archon, you are still the selfish, petulant child I remember," Morakar said. "We owe you nothing, *Crusher*. We only came to make sure, once Captain Burke is recovered, you can do no more damage."

"You mean to kill me?"

"The future of the Empire is bigger than any one person," Mazer said, standing. "You used to understand that. You once knew what honor and sacrifice in the service of our people were...but you threw it all away because of an unwholesome infatuation with a human. Your loyalty is to him over us, why should ours be to you over the Empire?"

"Then, let us settle this now," Crusher snarled. "By the old ways."

While Crusher had been talking Mazer and Morakar had risen and were moving to either side of him in an obvious flanking move. It was too obvious, and the brothers too cunning. They were up to something.

Growing impatient, Crusher launched off his left foot toward Mazer, who was the greater threat of the two. This strategy usually gave him a split-second element of surprise. This time, it did not. Perhaps *he* was too obvious. Morakar had launched himself at precisely the moment Crusher did, but from a stronger stance facing forward. He caught him just before Crusher would have reached Mazer, slamming into his back and tripping him up.

In a brilliant strategic move, Morakar rolled off to his left after the initial hit and cleared the way for Mazer to move in. Crusher had committed to rolling to counter Morakar as he fell and was helpless as he felt Mazer's claws rip into the skin of his shoulder, going deep but avoiding anything critical. Crusher roared in pain and sprang to his feet almost as soon as he touched the deck.

"It's too bad Doc didn't improve his brain while he was tinkering in there," Morakar remarked as he and his brother spread again to face him. "So strong, yet so, so stupid."

Crusher knew he needed to be analytical and fight like he had been trained, but his rage and bloodlust were surging and clouding his mind. It took all his self-control to not rush at them again. He narrowed his eyes and quieted his mind, letting them make the next move.

They didn't make him wait long.

. . .

Morakar lunged first, moving in close to the injured right arm. Crusher spun into the attack, slamming his left fist into Morakar's chin and driving a knee up into his midsection. Knowing Mazer would be coming, he dropped and rolled onto his back, raising his arms to guard his head. The other warrior had been coming at full speed for a takedown, and his shins bashed into Crusher's forearms, sending him flying and landing on top of his brother.

Before they could disentangle themselves, Crusher was on his feet and landed a well-placed kick to Mazer's ribs, hearing two crack. He grabbed the warrior by the legs and tossed him into some transit crates with enough force he hit the deck and stayed down. When Crusher turned back to Morakar, he saw the eldest Reddix still on the deck, dragging himself away and holding his hand up. He turned and saw that Mazer was struggling to sit up, leaning against the crates and holding his side.

"Please, go and see Doc about your injuries," Crusher said softly. "I will try to stay out of your way while you are still here. I understand your anger, but I will not fight two warriors I once considered friends and allies."

"Hold!" Mazer wheezed. "Crusher, please...stay."

"We apologize for the deception, my Lord," Morakar said. "But we had to be certain, and it had to seem real."

"I don't understand," Crusher said.

"We weren't sure what Doc had done to you. Even he wasn't," Morakar said. "What we knew was that the strength of your youth had been restored, but had your control remained? Young warriors spend the first quarter of their lives learning to rein in the powerful instincts that drive us to fight and kill. We were worried that, in his haste and ignorance, Doc might have returned you to a state where you would be too dangerous to be free."

"Ah," Crusher said, understanding dawning. "This was a test? But you could have been killed."

"That's a little insulting," Mazer said. "There *are* two of us and one of you."

"I'm aware," Crusher said.

"If we wanted you dead, a Zeta-Saka team would have been deployed discreetly from my office," Morakar said. "And you'd never see it coming. With Lucky and Jason missing, you were vulnerable. We came here in good faith to try and smooth this over in repayment for all you've done for us, but we had to be certain."

"They'll kill you, too, just for helping me," Crusher said quietly.

"Have some faith, my Lord," Mazer said, wincing as he stood. "We've done this sort of thing before."

"Let's drop this *lord* business," Crusher said. "I'm no longer the Guardian Archon. I'm not even Felex Tezakar. I'm just Crusher and, I hope, your friend."

"That's good," Mazer said. "Lord Archon Felex was an insufferable, arrogant asshole...but I've always liked Crusher."

"Go get yourselves patched up." Crusher laughed.

"What about you?" Morakar asked.

"What about me?" Crusher turned and showed them where his shoulder was already healed, just some fading thin lines in his dark skin to show where Mazer's claws had gotten him.

"I'll be damned," Mazer said in appreciation. "All that, and you get to look younger, too?"

"Don't even think about it," Morakar said.

"Worth a try," Mazer said. "Don't worry, Crusher...we'll handle this. Just so you know, you'll never be able to come home again, and you won't be interred in the Hall of Heroes."

"I understood the risks going in," Crusher said. "Well, mostly. Either way, I am committed to the path I have chosen."

"I think the treatment made him a bit smarter, too," Morakar said to his brother.

"Well, it couldn't have made him any dumber, that's for sure."

13

"The ship has dropped out of slip-space."

"Wonderful," Jason groaned. "Wake me up when something exciting happens."

"Do you intend to sleep through the entire voyage?" 701 asked.

"I know this won't make sense to you but, yes...I want to sleep. Against all odds, I actually have a comfortable rack on this ship, and who the hell knows what is coming up. I'm going to make sure I take the opportunity to sleep while I can."

A moment later, a siren blasted three times throughout the ship, signaling a muster in the main hold they had been brought into. Jason sighed and rolled out of his rack. They'd been in slip-space for the last six days and had lapsed into an easy routine of eating, sleeping, and avoiding any more fights. The three aliens that had accosted them at the beginning had never rejoined the main group, but Jason figured they must have been fully healed by now. He hoped they hadn't been tossed out an airlock for something so minor.

"Perhaps we will be told our mission now," 701 said.

"No chance," Jason said. "We're probably being dumped someplace to get geared up and begin training on whatever the mission is. If these guys are as smart and careful as they seem, it will be done in such a way that we can't gain too much knowledge about the target before we're actually there."

"You have done this before?"

"A time or two. Come on."

They were among the first to arrive at the main hold and, from the harsh vibrations coming through the deck, Jason could tell the ship was deorbiting in preparation to land. It was another twenty minutes before the entire group mustered, all of them looking surly and uncooperative. He looked around but still could not find the tall, blue-skinned trio that had assaulted him on the first day.

"Your attention," a modulated voice came from the bulkhead speakers.

"Who the hell are you?" someone yelled.

"I am the one who is paying you to do a job," the voice said. "You will soon be landing at a specialized training complex—"

"Called it," Jason said.

"—where you will be forged into a cohesive unit rather than a random collection of highly skilled operators. The job you have been hired to do will be dangerous and difficult, but you will be rewarded accordingly. In addition to the upfront pay you have already secured, you each will receive a triple share bonus upon successful completion of the mission."

The cheering and yelling drowned out whatever else the voice said as the mercs couldn't believe their good fortune. Jason and 701 just exchanged a look, both realizing that Ancula probably had no intention of letting any of them survive the mission long enough to collect their triple share. This was just an incentive to make sure they took the training and the mission seriously. Since these were all guild mercenaries, it probably didn't occur to them that they were being set up. Their guildmasters would have given them assurances and, normally, they'd be right. No way would a client dare use guild fighters for cannon fodder for fear of reprisals. Somehow, Ancula had found a way to isolate himself in a way that there wouldn't be any blowback.

It was another ninety minutes before the alarms started blaring to let them know touchdown was imminent. There was a harsh grinding of the landing gear deploying, and the vibrations through the deck became more pronounced as the retros fired. The hard thump and shudder through the ship announced their arrival to wherever the hell they'd been transported to.

"Off the ship! Get the hell off my ship!" the first officer bellowed before the ramp had even dropped all the way to the ground. The mercs, being the antisocial types very aware of their reputations, refused to hurry. It wasn't until the first flashbang was tossed at them before the crowd really got moving.

Once they were outside, the ramp slammed shut, and the ship lifted back off, the engines running to full power and tossing them around in the thruster wake. The troop transport pulled away so quickly that, in the mad rush, none of them had noticed they'd been dumped in the middle of nowhere. Others were still cussing and shaking their fist at the sky while Jason looked around in every direction, his limited helmet scanners picking up nothing.

"You got anything?" he asked.

"Nothing," 701 said. "We are isolated. How robust is your combat suit?"

"Softshell light armor with all the usual bells and whistles," Jason said. "Why?"

"Power levels?"

"Full. Why?"

"Because you will need it to regulate your body temperature if we are out at night," 701 said, looking around. "The delta between the ground temperature and the air temperature, which is rapidly falling, indicates this region will be cold during nighttime."

"Copy that," Jason said. "I'll adjust power allocation. Should give me two weeks, which is more than enough time."

"How do you know that?"

"Because I'll be dead from dehydration or lack of food before that," Jason said, turning to the group that was now showing signs of turning on itself. "Listen up!"

"Why should we listen to you?" someone shouted.

"You want to fight a battlesynth without any weapons?" Jason asked. That shut *everyone* up. "Any of you ever serve in a regular military? Raise your hands if you did." Most of the hands went up.

"This looks like one of those bullshit team building exercises they like to do. They drop us in the middle of nowhere and force us to pull together to survive. Or...we kill each other, and they go recruit another group from Enzola-2. Hell, we might not even be the first group."

"What do you think we should do since you're so smart?" the same loudmouth shouted. Jason made note of who it was.

"We're in a high desert on the southern hemisphere," Jason said. "My helmet sensors aren't good enough to give much more than that. We're in early evening, and the temperature is dropping. We need to find shelter first, food and water second. Anybody experienced in this sort of environment?"

"We are," a D'eltik said, motioning to her partner. Jason had limited experience with the species but, from what he knew, they were intelligent and dependable, not prone to bouts of stupidity or rage like Taukkir. "Our homeworld is mostly desert."

"Suggestions?" Jason asked. The pair exchanged a look, and then gazed around them.

"That way," she said finally. "We will want to follow the terrain downward and into what will hopefully be a valley. There will be better chance of water, prey, and possibly even natural barriers from the elements."

"Why should we listen to them?" loudmouth shouted again. Jason sighed and turned to him.

"You don't have to. You are welcome to just wait here and die. In your case, I would actually recommend it," Jason said, drawing a few laughs from the crowd.

"Where are the three that you two maimed early in this trip?" someone asked. "The triplets from Fumino Major."

"No idea." Jason shrugged. "If they're not here, they're probably still on the ship. Hopefully, not tossed out an airlock for something stupid like a fight. Everybody ready? We'll take it easy. Enough pace to keep everybody warm but not burn too many calories."

"You have managed to appoint yourself leader," 701 said as they took the lead.

"Yeah," Jason said. "Not optimal, I know. I've now got the biggest target on my back. In these situations, there's usually a lot of leadership turnover early on. If we don't find food and shelter tonight, they'll try to strangle me in my sleep."

"Then, why did you do it?"

"I was serious when I said they'll just leave us to die and go recruit another group. We won't be much use to the other two if I'm dead and you're stranded here."

"A valid point," 701 said. "Do not fear. I require no sleep and will allow no harm to come to you while you rest."

"What about when I'm awake?"

"You will fend for yourself."

Jason honestly couldn't tell if the battlesynth was joking or not. Lucky, Tin Man, and 784 all had reasonably developed senses of humor. 701 was dry as the hardpacked dirt beneath his boots and completely literal.

He boosted his sensors a bit to scan ahead, risking the power drain and hoping he might see something in the long-range thermals that would indicate shelter. Instead, he saw nothing but scrubby plants, a skeleton of some sort, and the dark shadow of the foothills in the distance. They were definitely moving downhill, but he saw no evidence of a valley or ravine ahead.

"Another factor to consider," 701 spoke again. "There might be agents within this group working for Ancula that will actively try to cause our failure."

"Yeah," Jason said, looking over his shoulder at Loudmouth. "I was thinking that myself."

"This seems to be a needless delay."

"We need to get them thinking and working as a unit before the actual mission training begins," Ancula said. "This is an accepted method to do that. Do you know that battlesynth down there?"

"I know every battlesynth," Lucky said. "That is 302. We have never worked together. His unit was used exclusively as VIP protection on Miressa Prime. I am not certain why he would be on Enzola-2 working as a mercenary."

"Perhaps he didn't want to go back home," Ancula said. "With the collapse Miressa's power and influence has now been eclipsed by Khepri. He could have been recalled and decided he wanted to travel the galaxy...as you once did."

"Suta's information regarding my departure may be somewhat inaccurate," Lucky said. "Clouded by his own bias."

"He informed me there was bad blood between you two from a long time ago. I must commend you for keeping it contained while you have been in my employ."

Lucky didn't see himself as an *employee* at the moment, but he said nothing.

On the large wall monitor, they were watching real-time imagery from a high-altitude observation drone of the group that had just been dumped in the desert. Ancula, who had never served in a combat unit, much less trained one, thought this ridiculous and dangerous stunt of leaving them stranded would build a cohesive team. Knowing mercs like he did, Lucky knew that it would be likely that the group would turn on itself sooner than later. At least Jason would have the protection of a fully armed battlesynth as an advantage.

"What are they doing?" Ancula asked.

"They are moving toward a lower elevation area likely in search of shelter," Lucky said. "The region you dropped them in will cool significantly during the night. Enough so that some of the species may struggle to survive in it."

"They will need to find a way," Ancula said, sounding annoyed that Lucky was questioning his methodology.

Lucky knew that his friends would have little trouble surviving on the surface. 701 was nearly invulnerable, and Jason had been wearing advanced light armor that would help him regulate his body temperature and would protect him from any potential attacks.

"What is the end goal of this exercise?" Lucky asked.

"To give us a better sense of who the stronger players are," Ancula said. "We only need about half of the number we have on the ground right now. We will observe them for a time and see how they react to less-than-optimal conditions."

Lucky again said nothing. He knew that each of the mercs down there was a highly trained, battle-hardened fighter or a skilled specialist. The point of using guild fighters was that they were already prescreened. Tormenting them like they were fresh recruits was just as likely going to get them to band together and try to kill you as it would forge them into a cohesive unit. More likely, in fact.

"You disagree with my methodology?" Ancula asked.

"That is not relevant," Lucky said. "I have been tasked with training a team for a mission, and that is what I will do to the best of my ability."

Ancula seemed to lose interest in the conversation and drifted back to the desk, leaving Lucky to watch the monitor. He didn't believe that this was simply some wilderness survival test. Something else was happening, or would happen, and Lucky couldn't determine what that might be.

"Come," Ancula said. "We have other things to attend to, and the computers will continue to keep an eye on them."

Lucky reluctantly turned to leave. It was difficult enough when he had to worry about Kage's safety. Now, Jason had inserted himself into this mess, and Lucky had yet one more variable to account for. At least Crusher and the others were safe on S'Tora.

14

"Who's next!!"

The large, multi-level hall was packed to the rafters, most of the patrons heavily intoxicated and watching the action below in the fighting ring where a young-looking Galvetic warrior had just beat two Korkarans almost to death. As the organizers dragged the victims from the ring, the big warrior eyed the crowd, daring anyone else to step in and fight him. This had been his fourth bout, and he was covered in blood, but none of it his own.

"I almost forgot how powerful he had been in his youth," Morakar said in an awed voice. "It's breathtaking."

"You have a lock on our target yet?" Mazer asked.

"Almost," Twingo said. "His personal com unit is definitely here, and it's active."

The group was on Enzola-2 looking for some idea where Jason and 701 might have gone. The SX-5 had been found sitting abandoned on the ramp at a starport near a city that catered to mercs and PMC contractors. The ship had been unmolested, but nothing inside offered any clues as to where they might have gone. Given the current state of their finances, Doc had secured long-term storage for the ship but didn't have her towed into a hangar. They didn't have time to ferry her out to wherever the *Devil's Fortune* might be, and she was far too expensive a piece of equipment to just leave for the scavengers.

It had taken five days on the *Phoenix* sending out feelers and searching through guild records to find the needle in the haystack. Doc and Twingo didn't bother trying to guess where Jason might have been or what he was doing. 701 was a much easier target given the rarity of the species outside of Khepri's military. Even then, it had taken some time before they learned that a battlesynth and another being listed as *species unknown* had walked into a brokerage looking for work. The broker had eagerly signed them up and vouched for them to get them onto the guild rolls. The commission he would make off a battlesynth alone would put him in easy living for some time on that world.

Now, it was just a matter of tracking down a squirrely broker with a lot of money keeping a low profile. It had been easy enough to figure out their target had a fondness for gambling on the fights and to hatch a plan to track him down through that. Rather than scour the dozens and dozens of fight houses within that city alone, they entered Crusher into one of the larger operations and let him begin building a reputation over the next few days. It was almost overnight that word got out about an unbeatable Galvetic fighter, and the place had been packed beyond capacity.

"Anything yet?" Mazer asked.

"I'm not Kage," Twingo said. "This isn't as simple a task as you're making it out to be."

"So...anything yet?" Mazer repeated. Twingo sighed and kept scanning. The device he was using could pick out individual com units that were linked to the public Nexus, but it didn't give a pinpoint location since com units only connected at irregular intervals.

"Second, no...first tier," Twingo said. "Northwest corner. Doc?"

"Looking now," Doc said over the com. He was at the rail of the third tier with a good view of everything except what was directly below him. "Nothing standing out."

"Sending his com unit a hit now," Twingo said. "See if he jumps or checks it."

"Got him," Doc said. "Shorter Eshquarian—"

"Shorter than what?" Mazer asked.

"Shorter than me," Doc snapped. "He's wearing a dark gray coat over blue overalls."

"Stylish," Twingo said. "What's he doing?"

"He looks panicked after that random hit you sent his com unit. His head is on a swivel, and he's moving toward the cashier counter. Probably cashing out and bolting."

"I've got eyes on him," Mazer said, looking up and spotting the target.

"Moving outside now," Morakar said. "Twingo, you're on Crusher duty."

"What the hell is that?"

"When we grab the target, you'll have to tell him the fun is over, and he needs to leave."

"Shit."

───────

Skalyt knew he had been spotted.

Well, maybe he didn't *know*, but his instincts were screaming that the Galvetic warrior wearing the ridiculous hooded garment to hide his bulk had been staring at him far too intently. He knew the gambling houses hired competent enforcers, but *Galvetic warriors?!* That seemed excessive for someone who was only down...what? Maybe forty thousand credits? That hardly seemed worth sending that monster after him.

"Hurry!"

"I am going as quickly as the system allows, sir."

Skalyt wanted to punch the cashier in the face as he slowly loaded his winnings onto five credit chits.

"You sure you don't want to stay for the main—"

"Shut your mouth and give me my credits!" Skalyt yelled, much louder than he'd intended. Now, everyone in the line was staring at him.

"Here, sir. I apologize for the wait."

Skalyt ripped the chits from his hands and fled. There was a back staircase hardly anybody ever used that went straight to a door that would put him near the service entrances. From there, he could blend in with the rest of the staff and get back to his domicile.

There! The stairs were just ahead, and the Galvetic was nowhere in sight. He made it through the archway and was flying down the stairs, his heart racing. He'd had to elude enforcers a time or two, and it seemed he was getting pretty good at it. By the time he got to the door, he was almost smiling, certain that he'd be able to get away tonight and deal with the problem tomorrow. Or maybe the day after.

"Going somewhere?" a deep voice rumbled from behind him after he'd made it outside.

He yelped and broke into a sprint. Or at least he tried to. A clawed hand that felt like a steel vise clamped onto his shoulder and squeezed hard enough that his legs gave out from under him.

"I have the money! I swear! Just give me a day to get it all together!"

"I have the target," the Galvetic said, ignoring him. "Coming to you."

"You're going to kill me, aren't you?" Skalyt said quietly, his eyes darting about wildly looking for anyone who might help him. But this was Enzola-2. Nobody was going to help him. They just pretended not to see and went quickly about their business.

"Maybe we can work out some kind of—"

"You talk a lot for someone who has no idea what they've gotten themselves into," the warrior growled. "If you wish to survive the next ten minutes, you should stay silent."

———————

"Thanks for not ripping my head off when I told you it was time to go," Twingo said.

"Thank you for asking nicely," Crusher replied. "I know I've threatened to kill you a lot over the years, but I was mostly kidding."

"Comforting," Twingo said sourly.

The pair had cashed out Crusher's winnings, a hefty sum even minus Twingo's twenty percent as his manager and had left to the boos of the crowd who had packed into the place to see the next fight. The rest of the team waited with the guild broker in a rental unit that had both living quarters and a workspace of the type that was common in cities that catered to transients. Thankfully, it was a short walk from the entertainment district.

"You looked good," Twingo said as they walked. "Took me back years ago when you would take on two or three at a time and win."

"I feel good. I only wish it hadn't come with such a steep price."

"Do you regret it?"

"No," Crusher said after some thought. "Not going back to Restaria stings a bit, but the thought of letting you guys down was a crushing pain I couldn't bear. We started this thing together all that time ago. I want to be healthy enough to see it to the end."

"You realize the end will probably be us all dying in that gunship when it gets blown out of the sky, right?" Twingo asked.

"Then, I'll be there with you for that, too."

They arrived at the rental unit after taking a few turns and cutbacks to see if they were followed and were let inside by Morakar. The broker was tied to a chair, and Mazer entertained himself by showing the captive all the different blades he'd brought with him.

"We get anything yet?" Crusher asked.

"You?" the broker asked, confused. "Why would you be here? Hey! Are the Nuntir Brothers fixing the fights?"

"Huh?" Twingo asked.

"He thinks we are enforcers for one of the gambling houses he owes a significant debt to," Morakar said. "Now, we know which one."

"That makes things easier," Crusher said.

"If I reported you to—"

"Silence!" Crusher barked.

"How do you want to do this?" Doc asked. "He is a guild broker, so we can't exactly leave him broken and bloody in the streets."

"True," Crusher agreed. "Better to just kill him outright to be safe."

"Not what I meant."

"Who are you guys?"

"Let's start with who you are," Doc said. "We know your name is Skalyt and that you're a contract broker for the local mercenary guilds. Give us the information we need, and we'll leave. Maybe we'll even make it worth your while."

"No. Oh, no. No, no, no. There is *no* way I'm going to divulge any guild contract details. The Nuntir Brothers might kill me for owing them, the guilds would put my brain in a jar and keep it alive for years just to torture me as long as possible."

"What if we paid your debt off to these Nuntir Brothers?" Doc asked.

"Not a chance would I... Wait, the *whole* debt?"

"What do you owe to get back to zero?"

"Well, I've had a bit of an unlucky streak lately and it's been—"

"The number!" Crusher snarled.

"One hundred and thirty thousand credits!" Skalyt said. "Forty by tomorrow if I want to keep my hands."

"How much money did you make tonight?" Doc asked Crusher.

"What?! Fuck you! I'm not giving this little gambling junkie my winnings!" Crusher said hotly.

"Money is tight right now." Doc shrugged. "We all need to make personal sacrifices for the greater good. How much?"

"A little over one-eighty," Crusher mumbled.

"You made almost two hundred thousand in one night beating up Korkarans?" Mazer asked. "I'm in the wrong business."

"You're also too old and fat," Morakar said.

"That, too."

"If your information isn't good, I will find a way to get my money's worth out of you," Crusher growled, leaning down into Skalyt's face.

"It is! I mean, it probably is. I actually have no idea what you people want."

"We're looking for the details on a contract one of the guilds you broker for helped fill," Doc said. "This should be easy for you to remember since one of the people who signed on was a battlesynth."

"Ah...that one," Skalyt said, squirming.

"And?" Mazer asked.

"Look...I can get in a lot of trouble here. This is a tricky situation."

"Trickier than being tired to a chair and having a Galvetic warrior waiting eagerly to disembowel you for costing him money?" Doc asked.

"I see your point. The battlesynth came to me and asked that he be given a spot on that contract for himself and his companion, some alien wearing full gear and a helmet," Skalyt said. "That meant I had to forge their guild credentials to even get them in the building for the selection process. I really can't say more. If I get caught doing that—"

"Disembowelment," Doc reminded him.

"Right, right. So, I get them the paperwork that says they're from a small but still-accredited guild out in the Concordian Cluster. Truth is, it actually only exists on a computer for another purpose, but it was a passable workaround. I mean...he's a damn battlesynth, so it's not like he can't fight."

"Then what?" Twingo asked.

"They went with the other candidates and both ended up selected and taken off-world," Skalyt said. "The selection process was strange. Some black kill-bot named Seven was in charge of determining who was picked, but all he did was ask random questions."

"Gonna need more to keep your insides on the inside," Crusher said. "Details on the contract. Who hired them and for what purpose?"

"No idea. Contract was executed through layers of dummy corporations. The best I can do is get you the information on the transport they hired to move them. The contract holder didn't use their own ship."

"We'll take that," Twingo said. "And we'll also take what you're holding out on."

"Don't know what you mean."

"You know more than you're saying," Mazer said. "And we're going to get it out of you." Skalyt looked from person to person in the room before going on, apparently satisfied that they would indeed do what they threatened to do.

"Rumor is the contract was initiated by a company that is a suspected front for some Vissalo moneyman," he said. "He's supposedly part of the M'aqu Crime Family, but he's usually operated on the clean end of their businesses. It's been the subject of much speculation what someone like that would need such a sizable merc force for and why he was taking such trouble to isolate himself from it."

"Cut him loose and pay him," Doc said. "We have what we need."

Mazer cut the straps holding him to the chair, and Crusher slapped a small case with the credit chits into his hand.

"No lecture on how I should go straight to the gambling houses and clear my name? Skalyt asked with a smirk.

"I paid you for the information. What you do with it is up to you. Shove it up your ass sideways for all I care," Crusher said. "Just as long as whatever you do is out of my sight."

Skalyt wasted no time getting out of the unit and disappearing into the night.

"He'll be heading right back to the fights and will probably lose it all," Twingo said. "You know that, right?"

"Honestly, if he does and the people he owes kill him, the better for us. He's a loose end," Crusher said.

"Brutal, but practical," Mazer said. "What's next?"

"Now, we dig into this Vissalo and find out why Lucky is down here hiring a merc army for him," Doc said. "It sounds like the captain has managed to get himself captured so this just got a lot more interesting."

"These guys always have way more fun than we do," Mazer said to his brother, who only rolled his eyes and sighed.

15

"Are you awake?"

"Yes," Jason said.

"Three figures are approaching from the far ridge. They are heavily armed."

Jason rolled up to a sitting position and commanded his suit's long-range sensors to maximum, risking the power drain to get an idea of what was coming for them. He immediately recognized them even in the monochromatic image of the thermal sensors.

"You've got to be shitting me," he muttered.

"Indeed," 701 said. "Your friends have been given powerful weapons and apparently sent to harass us."

The mercenaries were sleeping in groups of four or five to conserve body heat within the low-ceilinged cave they had found. They had been exhausted by the time they reached it, so nobody complained about a lack of food or water. That would undoubtedly begin in the morning. 701 had been keeping watch, but Jason had been drifting in and out of a light sleep as he didn't need to expend as much energy keeping warm as the others.

"I'm not detecting any gear except the weapons," Jason said.

"Neither am I."

"This group is likely to kill our employer the first chance they get for putting them through this."

"A possibility."

"Okay," Jason said, standing up and stretching. "Let's go get 'em. I'll drop down to the ravine floor and wait for them to make their crossing by that eroded section to the right of us."

"I will wait farther uphill and observe in case they do not cross there," 701 said.

They slipped away into the night, moving slowly to maintain a silent approach across the loose stones scrub. A few moments later, they lost line of sight of their targets, so Jason switched off his long-range sensors to conserve power. In the low-light amplification his helmet provided, he was able to pick his way carefully down until he reached the part of the ravine worn smooth by regular flooding and could take off at a quick run.

Jason settled into the small nook in the rocks and waited where he was sure the assault team would come. It was the most logical place to make it down to the ravine bed from the steeper, more treacherous side they were descending. He boosted the gain on his auditory sensors and was able to hear them slipping and cursing as they descended.

"We just get close enough to shoot the one who injured me," one was saying. "Don't get close enough to let the battlesynth shoot back. They have a short effective range."

Jason knew that wasn't actually true, but it was interesting that they thought so. Most of what people thought they knew of 701's species was rumor and myth, a lot of it put out by the Kheprian Ministry of Martial Affairs itself. From working with Lucky all those years, he knew they were already well within 701's effective kill range.

"What if it chases us?" another asked.

"It won't," the first said confidently. "It will tend to its friend. By the time the group figures out what happened, we'll already have been picked up."

Jason was able to figure out that the three morons had been given weapons and set upon them by their employer, ostensibly to create chaos to see how they'd react. They must have been fed a load of shit about battlesynth capabilities and behavior since Ancula would know damn well that 701 would kill all three even if he hadn't seen them coming four klicks away.

The rocks sliding down and bouncing off his helmet was the first warning they were close. He tensed up and watched to his left, waiting to see the first of them, so he was startled when he heard a muffled curse, some sliding, and then a loud *thud* right in front of him as one of the enemy slid over the drop off. It groaned and clutched at its shoulder, not seeing Jason.

"Hey there," Jason said softly. It turned to look at him, gawking as he seemed to materialize out of the dark before kicking him in the face as hard as he could. The alien's head snapped back, and there was a wet crunching sound, so he wasn't entirely sure he hadn't killed it.

"M'nes?" a harsh whisper called. "Are you okay?" Jason groaned with what he hoped was close to the noise he'd heard the alien make as he slipped over and collected the weapon. It was a heavy plasma rifle of the same make Crusher had a fondness for. He checked the status, and then slunk back into the shadows.

"We need to get down there and help him."

"Of course, we do, but I don't want to land on top of him by making the same misstep. There! Take that worn path to your left. It leads all the way down."

The wait wasn't long before the two came bumbling around the corner, focused entirely on their friend. He let them get closer before he stepped out, weapon raised. As he did, 701 emerged from cover, switching to combat mode and firing his repulsors, slamming down in the ravine bed behind them. His glowing red eyes lit up the narrow ravine as he trained his arm cannons on them.

"Lose the weapons," Jason said. "Now! Toss them away."

"You!" the taller one hissed.

"Don't," Jason warned him, but it was too late. The alien tried to raise his weapon, but Jason was faster. He squeezed the trigger and vaporized his enemy's head. The body convulsed and the weapon it still held fired, the plasma bolt hitting in front of Jason's feet and kicking up bits of molten rock that hissed on the outer layer of his armor. He was momentarily disoriented and vulnerable, but 701 wasn't. The battlesynth shot the third assailant before Jason could even bring his weapon to bear.

"The others will have heard the weapons fire," 701 said.

"I'm keeping this one, destroy the other two," Jason said. "For now, I'll feel better being the only one armed until we figure out what this sadistic game is all about."

701 disabled both weapons by venting the plasma charge and breaking both over his knee, throwing the remnants far out into the desert.

"Better if the others think there was only one weapon between the three of them, not that you decided to destroy the rest," he explained.

"Smart," Jason said. "Hey, this one is still alive."

Jason knelt near the one he'd hit first, shaking him gently.

"W-what hap—"

"You were sent to attack the rest of the group," Jason said, sensing there wasn't a lot of time left to get answers. "You fell down that cliff. What were you told to do?"

"My brothers?"

"No idea where they went," Jason lied, trying to keep him focused. "Answer the question, please."

"We were supposed to attack the group."

"Why?"

"Don't...know."

"Were you supposed to kill or just engage?"

"They didn't say. Just gave us weapons and..." His head slumped over, and he stopped breathing. Jason stared at him a moment longer before rising to his feet.

"Think they just tossed them out to create chaos to see how we'd react?" he asked.

"Possible," 701 said. "Nothing about this contract has made sense, but I will admit to not being as experienced at this sort of thing as you are."

"No, you're absolutely right," Jason said. "This is the weirdest thing I've ever heard about. Nobody in their right mind goes through the trouble of hiring pros for a job, and then screws with them like this before the job even starts. This is the crap militaries do, but half these mercs will walk at the first chance or try to kill whoever put them here."

"There is movement from the encampment."

Jason looked up as four members of the group came sliding down the hill. They slowed down and approached with caution when they saw Jason holding the heavy plasma rifle.

"What happened here?"

"Looks like these three were turned loose with a weapon to attack us in the night," Jason said. "We intercepted them."

"How did you know they were coming?" another asked suspiciously.

"I have the ability to scan this entire valley," 701 said. "I saw them coming and alerted my partner."

"Don't you think we should talk about who gets that gun?" the first asked, nodding to the plasma rifle.

"We already did," Jason said. "We took a vote, but you weren't here for it. The gun stays with me."

"Now what?" the second asked.

"For now, I say we stop playing whatever stupid game this is," Jason said. "So long as nobody starts eating any of the others, we should stay put until we're collected."

"If we're not?"

"Then, I guess try to pick out someone who looks like they might taste good."

"That didn't work like I had hoped."

"I warned you," Lucky said.

"To be honest, this was Suta's idea," Ancula said, glaring at Suta where he stood in the corner. "He disagreed with using mercs and convinced me that it would be best to stress test them prior to the mission to weed out the weaklings. The night attack was supposed to force them to rally together, not be defeated before it started."

"They were never going to get close with a battlesynth keeping watch through the night," Lucky said. "Perhaps we should make our selections and move ahead with the mission."

"Perhaps," Ancula admitted. "We aren't too close on time, but it would be better to have the pieces ready and in place to make sure there are no missteps."

Suta remained silent, glowering at Lucky. They had been watching the footage recorded during the night and saw that the assault team Ancula had assumed would thin the herd had been neutralized with embarrassing ease. Lucky was concerned that the incident would make Jason and 701 stand out from the crowd too much. So far, neither Ancula nor Suta gave any indication they knew who either of them really were, but he didn't want them under increased scrutiny.

"You brought me here to do a job," Lucky said. "Please, let me do it."

"The job you were brought here to do is one you can no longer even perform," Suta said.

"I am the best chance you have of training a group in a short amount of time to do a specific mission," Lucky countered. "And you well know it."

"Quiet. Both of you," Ancula said, staring out the window at the planet below. "Suta, take a security detail down to the surface and collect the mercs. Make sure they disarm that one." He pointed to the frozen image of Jason Burke killing one of the assailants.

"What do you wish done with them?" Suta asked.

"Simply have them on the transport. We will be leaving for

Arospor-4 at once," Ancula said. "We will begin the operational phase of this mission."

"At once," Suta said, turning and leaving.

"You will have a short span of time to select your team and execute a raid on a fortified location," Ancula said. "We will need to acquire certain...leverage. Once that is complete, we can move on to our primary objective."

"I will make certain we succeed," Lucky said.

"See that you do," Ancula said. "That is all."

Lucky swiftly left the suite, intent on visiting Kage before Suta came back to the ship. They had much to discuss and very little time to do it in. He had been keeping his distance to make sure Suta didn't become suspicious and find out that Kage had fully recovered. If his friend was tossed in a holding cell, it would take him off the board completely.

Suta's ridiculous experiment on the surface of the planet below had cost them time, and Lucky had already spent more of that in his company than he would have liked. For some reason, the crime boss seemed reluctant to take that final step and actually execute his plan even after carefully gathering all the pieces. Lucky wished he knew what made him so hesitant, but he suspected they were all about to anger someone much worse than Ancula himself given how much effort had been put into isolating himself from the operation.

Time. It was all about time. Or, more accurately, the lack of it. Lucky was running out of time to make sure all of his friends made it out of this mess alive.

16

"It looks like you were right," one of the mercs said as they filed back onto the transport.

"Pretty easy guess," Jason said. "Hard to believe someone would pay guild prices for a bunch of mercs to leave them out in the desert for too long."

When the ship had landed, and a squad of heavily armed troopers came out, Jason had been ordered to surrender his weapon immediately. He could only laugh as they knew he was partnered with a battlesynth who had ten times the firepower of that single weapon with him at all times, yet they seemed unconcerned about letting him onto the ship.

There was a strange looking synth with armor and weapons bolted to itself that caught Jason's eye, but only because it was looking at 701 with an intensity that made him uncomfortable. Thankfully, some of their fellow mercs provided a distraction. Apparently, they were still quite angry and being left out in the desert hungry and cold all night, and a group of eleven attacked the security troopers. In the ensuing chaos, Jason and 701 were able to slip onto the ship and go back to berthing while the strange synth helped subdue the combatants.

"Who—*what*—the hell was that thing?" Jason asked once he and 701 were alone.

"He is called Combat Unit P002," 701 said. "I am surprised to see him still alive. He is not supposed to be."

"What is the P designation for?"

"Prototype. When the idea to weaponize synths was finally accepted by the Ministry of Martial Affairs, the program office originally thought they could just up-armor and arm standard synths to get the results they were after. When that was met with poor results, the battlesynth program was authorized, and purpose-built military units were designed."

"But he's still around?" Jason asked.

"He was supposed to have been dismantled and his matrix destroyed," 701 said.

"How do you know that?"

"I was there. I was there with 707 and 777 on the mission when P002 went insane and killed hundreds of civilians. We were told by our superiors that he would be destroyed for his crimes."

"Whoa," Jason said. "I think I've heard part of this story."

"I am certain you have. The incident was the catalyst for Lucky leaving."

"Would this guy recognize you?" Jason asked, concerned their cover was blown.

"Unlikely," 701 said. "Our appearances were altered when our master, Krunt Teludal, hid us on his estate. I believe you met him before finding us buried in stasis pods."

"Yeah, I remember him," Jason said, thinking back to their mission on Khepri. It brought up unpleasant memories. Memories of Lucky dying trying to protect him.

"P002 will not recognize me by sight, and I am sure Lucky will have given them a false name if they asked him who I am," 701 said.

"That's something, I suppose. It's starting to come back to me about how Teludal took all of you out of the system and off the grid. I guess it would make sense he'd alter your physical appearance as well."

They fell silent. The deck shook as the thrusters fired, and the ship prepared to lift. Jason's thoughts were wrapped around this new bit of information and how best to use it to his advantage, or at least not let it bite him in the ass. He knew nothing about this P002 since Lucky had never given much detail about that time of his life.

"You guys hear what happened?" one of the mercs popped their head into the cramped quarters.

"About?" Jason asked.

"That crazy looking synth killed eleven guild mercs out there. It said if any of us retaliate, it'll kill all of us, too."

"Well," Jason said. "That's not something we can just let stand, is it?"

"No, it isn't. Glad to see we're in agreement."

"Ping the others. Quietly. Let's make sure we're all on the same page."

"Will do," the merc said, disappearing.

"It appears you have found your angle," 701 said.

"What are you talking about?"

"Unless I missed my mark, the look of concentration on your face a moment ago indicated you were working out how to turn P002's presence to your advantage."

"*Our* advantage, but yes…that's what I was thinking."

"And?"

"And I think once they arm us for this mission, things will get very interesting," Jason said. "But I'm not sure that helps us. At least not yet."

"The captain and 701 are here. They managed to get themselves aboard the troop transport by posing as mercs vying for a contract slot."

"Not good," Kage said through the link. "Any luck on getting me out of here?"

"It is a bit difficult when you are pretending to be incapacitated. So, no," Lucky said.

"Fair point. What do we do now?"

"I will try to find an opportunity to confer with the captain and see what his plan might have been."

"You know it was some stupid shit that wouldn't have worked anyway," Kage said. "But if you just let him go, somehow he'll make it work."

"701 will not allow him to freelance without some plan of action for too long," Lucky said.

"You have any idea who we're supposed to be breaking out of prison? If it's the sort of place Ancula can't buy his way into, it may not be the sort of place you and Jason can fight your way into either."

"I have considered that. But our choices are—"

"Lucky! Master Ancula has been trying to contact you!"

Lucky turned and saw one of the orderlies who served Ancula in the executive suite.

"I have been here with my friend." Lucky toward Kage, who was pretending to be asleep. "Is there an emergency?"

"You could say that. The troop transport has just made orbit. Suta killed eleven of the mercs on the surface."

"I see," Lucky said. "Lead the way, please."

The orderly led him directly to Ancula's operations center on the command deck. The Vissalo himself was angry and pacing while his operators talked to the transport ship. When he saw Lucky, he stopped pacing and walked over to him.

"We have a problem. Eleven mercs died on the surface," he said.

"That is an occupational hazard," Lucky said, playing dumb. "Did you not want to reduce the size of your force before the mission began?"

"Not necessarily, I just wanted them working a little better together than a group of hired guns who had never met," Ancula said. "But this is a bit different. Suta killed them on the ramp of the ship in broad view of everyone."

"The guilds will not view that as an acceptable combat death," Lucky warned.

"And Suta is known to be in my employ," Ancula said. "He is too unique a creature for nobody to have recognized him or accurately describe him to someone who would."

"Unfortunately, the traits that make him useful to you also make him a liability," Lucky said. "Is he still on the transport ship?"

"He's isolated on the command deck while what remains of the security detail keeps order," Ancula said. "Thankfully, that battlesynth appeared to have no interest in the fray. The captain of the ship said he simply went back to berthing with his partner."

"He was not being paid to attack your crew," Lucky said. "He would have suffered no discomfort during your test, so he would have no interest in getting revenge."

"This is an unexpected complication, but nothing that we can't handle," Ancula said. "I'm sure the guilds can be reasoned with for the right price."

Lucky knew better but said nothing. The merc guilds did value money above almost everything else. Everything except their honor. Once they found out that Ancula had hired them through a straw buyer, and then one of his goons killed a bunch of them they would take it personally. From a practical point of view, they couldn't afford for their members or their customers to see them tolerating someone killing their fighters for sport.

"We should depart the area quickly," he said. "You hired pros. Let them do their jobs. They will fight to the death for the money you paid them, there is no need to try and turn them into something they are not."

"I should have listened to you from the beginning," Ancula said quietly. He looked over at his com operators and raised his voice. "Inform the transport that Suta will be remaining aboard as a guest. He is not to interact with the contractors in any way. Make certain he understands that."

"Yes, sir."

"Tell the captain that he may set course for Arospor-4 at his discretion," Ancula said. "And make sure the transport makes it there ahead of us. Lucky, please come with me."

Lucky followed his abductor out of the operations center and down the corridor to his private suite. At first, he was happy to try and fill the role of confidant to gain an advantage over Ancula but, recently, he'd begun to resent that the Vissalo treated him as a friend despite holding him and Kage here against their wills.

"You probably won't like this next part," Ancula said as he went straight to the sidebar to make himself a drink.

"No offense, but I have not liked any part of this situation so far."

"We need to acquire leverage over someone," Ancula went on, ignoring Lucky. "That means abducting someone against their will, but it is absolutely critical that they not be harmed in any way. In fact, I will kill whoever does whether it is an accident or not."

"It seems you have hired a group of hammers when what you needed was a scalpel," Lucky said. "The mercs you had me screen—"

"Are for the main job," Ancula waved him off. "This is something I need the best for. I need you."

"The target will not be harmed in any way? Ever?"

"Not by my hand, and not by anyone working for me. I know my word means little to you, but I swear on my life that no harm will come to them."

"Would it be possible to pull from the mercs to execute this mission?" Lucky asked. "I would only need a few."

"The battlesynth," Ancula guessed. "Why do I feel like it would be dangerous to let the two of you loose together?"

"You still have Kage," Lucky pointed out. "My loyalty is to him. If Combat Unit 302 tried something that would put Kage's life in jeopardy, I would kill him."

"Can your new body take down a first generation battlesynth?"

"With ease."

"Very well. I will brief you on the target, and then you will be allowed to choose your personnel. Choose wisely."

"Understood."

17

"This doesn't make sense. This Ancula isn't usually the type of criminal who uses merc armies. This is a money guy who knows how to raise, move, and hide cash. Now, all of the sudden, he wants to play gangster?"

"Keep digging," Crusher grunted.

"This sucks without Kage," Twingo said, going back to browsing through the entries on the Zadra Network pertaining to Ancula. The first problem had been that they only had one name to go by, and Vissalo had five names that fully identified them. The next problem was that the Vissalo crime organizations were damn near airtight with very little intel making its way out.

They caught a break when Doc found a profile on the Vaiccr Syndicate that operated in the same region they suspected Ancula was from. It was a Vissalo organization that seemed to be controlled by two dominant families. Ancula was one of the main money men, pulling in all of the illicit cash from the families, filtering it through his operation, and making it available on the other side as clean. He had some small security force to protect major assets as well as himself, but nothing that would indicate why he would need to be on Enzola-2 hiring such a large group of specialized contractors.

"Listen to this," Mazer said, spinning his seat around. "Apparently there was an attempted coup within the Vaiccr Syndicate not all that long ago. One of the families decided to try and take over the entire operation by force. They lost, and the other family took steps to make sure they couldn't try something like that again, but they had to do it in a way that would ensure their operation didn't take any hits."

"Makes sense. Internal conflicts like that attract predators. Large syndicates are always under threat of outsiders wanting to move in on what they have," Twingo said. "Saditava Mok was the only person I've ever heard of who managed to keep an operation the size of Blazing Sun from imploding or fracturing."

"That he made it out alive is even more impressive," Crusher said. "Anything else, Mazer?"

"Oh, wow. It looks like the losing family in that little civil war were mostly killed off, but others were imprisoned," Mazer said. "I guess that was an insurance policy to keep the others in line."

"What others? You said they killed most of them," Doc pointed out.

"Only the ringleaders of the coup attempt," Mazer said. "And their underlings."

"You know something else." Crusher narrowed his eyes. "You're usually not this much of a storyteller."

"Want to know the name of one of the survivors of the losing side?" Mazer smiled.

"That's it," Morakar said, the first time he'd spoken in hours. Actually, Twingo had just assumed he was asleep at the bridge station. "That's what Ancula is after."

"Revenge?" Crusher snorted. "Not with a handful of mercs he's not."

"Of course not," Morakar said. "He doesn't have enough people to take out any of the higher ups...but maybe he has enough to break his family out of wherever they're being held."

"Does that report say?" Crusher asked.

"No," Mazer said.

"Then, what the hell use are you?"

"I'm back to wanting to kill him again," Mazer said to his brother. "Quick. Easy. We'll be back home within the week."

"Let's hold off on killing anybody until we're sure we don't need them," Doc said. "What's our best chance of finding where these people are being held at? I have a feeling if we get there soon enough, we'll find the others."

"That will be no small feat," Morakar said. "That information would have been kept secret even from Ancula himself. They wouldn't want him to be tempted to do something foolish as he appears ready to do."

"You guys hear that beeping?" Doc asked.

"I thought that was your terminal," Twingo said. "I've been hearing it for the last hour."

"Well...what is it?" Crusher demanded. Twingo sighed and got out of his seat.

"I have no idea. I put this damn thing back together in half the time I actually needed. Some shortcuts needed to be taken."

"That's comforting considering I'm riding on this antique with you," Mazer remarked.

Twingo walked around the bridge, listening for the intermittent beep before he realized it was coming from the com room. When he walked in, he saw that one of their emergency slip-com nodes on S'Tora had been receiving an incoming channel request. The slip-com array was in the hangar base, now in the hands of the S'Toran government. Didn't he purge those?

"What is it?" Doc called.

"Someone is pinging the emergency array on S'Tora," Twingo said, looking closer at the address. "Wait! No, it's one of Kage's. It's one of the backup systems he installed on the farm property."

"Who would know that address?" Doc asked, appearing at the hatchway.

"Only us," Twingo said. "This was something he was setting up on the chance the hangar base was compromised, but he never gave me the damn access codes. I can see we have a message, but I can't get to it."

"That has to be Kage himself accessing that, hoping you'll see it," Doc said.

"Still doesn't help," Twingo said helplessly. "He never loaded the current access codes into the *Phoenix*'s new computer. I could try and force my way in with that intrusion software package Voq designed, but then I run the risk of hitting one of Kage's failsafes and wiping the node on the remote end."

"He would have made it something you know," Doc said. "Do you still have the data from the *Phoenix*'s old computer cores?"

"Not in an easily accessible form," Twingo said, settling into the seat. "Give me a little time here. I'll try a few things, press in around the edges, and see what happens."

"Something is wrong."

"You are certain?" Lucky asked.

"All of the emergency slip-com nodes in the hangar are offline," Kage said. "I'm pinging one of my backups, but Twingo either doesn't see it or can't access it."

"The *Phoenix*?"

"I don't want to access her nodes directly. I'm time-sharing with a low-bandwidth node I could access from here on this ship, but there's a real risk of being discovered. I have to be careful what I send and where to."

"Understood."

"What's the play?"

"I think it is time for you to begin recovering. I will keep you out of detainment as long as possible, but you have done all you can from your comatose act."

"Copy that."

"I have to go. Ancula is expecting me."

Lucky broke the connection and left the infirmary without a word to the medical staff. He knew that they were aware of Kage being fully recovered, but they chose to say nothing. Lucky didn't want to put them at risk by acknowledging them and causing one of Ancula's ever-present security troopers to look more closely.

As he walked the corridors of the ship, he looked closely at those he passed. There was definitely the resentment of a crew that wasn't there of their own volition, but how was that even possible? How could Ancula crew a whole ship with conscripts? Spaceflight was *the* main industry in the galactic quadrant. Countless crews of spacers were available for hire who could fly any given ship in any given scenario. That would have to be cheaper—not to mention safer—than having a ship full of people who would rather kill you than follow your orders.

"Good afternoon," he said in greeting as he walked into Ancula's personal suite without the guards even giving him a second glance. Lucky almost thought he could neutralize the Vissalo and affect an escape, but Ancula was too smart to leave such an obvious vulnerability open...wasn't he?

"Lucky. Precisely on time as usual," Ancula said. "Let's begin."

As Lucky had feared, their mission included the abduction of a civilian. A young Vissalo female. She was in a secure compound, but hardly an impregnable one. Ancula was adamant that she was not to be harmed in any way, shape, or form, but he did say she wouldn't come willingly.

"May I impose on you to have your medical staff prepare a suitable tranquilizer for a Vissalo of her size?" Lucky asked mid-brief.

"Certainly," Ancula said. "You really think that is the preferred method?"

"Yes. If she is not going to come willingly, the risk of her injuring herself by resisting is quite high. We can subdue her, even if only partially, and then simply carry her out."

"You can carry her while possibly meeting armed resistance on the way back out to the extraction point?"

"I have done this many times. There are mitigating steps I will take to ensure that, even if we are engaged, she is reasonably protected. Normally, if a subject is under protection, they will not fire due to the risk of their ward," Lucky said. "I will not need a large team to do this if your intel on the compound is accurate."

"It's accurate," Ancula said. "How many do you need?"

"Only two. The battlesynth and his partner. They already work as a team, and the battlesynth can provide both protection and the strength to escape with the subject should I be incapacitated or killed."

"I'd prefer for you not to die," Ancula said. "Despite the circumstances of our association, I have grown rather fond of you." He stared at the holograph of the female for a long moment. "You're sure you can bring her out safely? Absolutely certain?"

"Nothing is absolute in this universe, but I can assure that if your intel is accurate, and they are not expecting us, we can capture and extract her with a high probability of success."

"How high?"

"Ninety-seven-point-eight."

"That's high," Ancula agreed. "Very well. I will have your new teammates brought over. You will depart from this ship aboard a small combat shuttle that I assume you are proficient to pilot."

"I am."

"Don't you want to know which type?"

"Unimportant," Lucky said. "If I might be so bold...this woman seems important to you in more ways than just a means to an end. If just crashing into the compound and dragging her out without a care was acceptable, you could just send Suta."

"She's important to me," Ancula said quietly. "And to many others as well. Involving her is not something I am at all proud of, but we do what we must in order to accomplish what is required of us. If there was any other way I could do this, I would."

"Thank you for answering," Lucky said. Ancula looked at him quizzically. "While Seven may have been a ruthless, brutal assassin, I am not. I prefer to have strong moral ground under me when I execute a mission. I appreciate that you are not sending me to kill or harm an innocent."

"I really wish we had met under different circumstances, Lucky," Ancula sighed. "We might have gotten along quite well."

"I will begin planning my assault," Lucky said. "Is there some-place I can review the intelligence on the compound in detail?"

"Use the operations center," Ancula said. "They'll provide anything you need."

"Very well. If you will excuse me?"

Ancula nodded over his shoulder at him but said nothing else. Lucky turned and left the executive suite, now more confused than before about who Ancula really was. His patterns of behavior simply didn't fit with a ruthless crime lord, but more of a desperate man backed into a corner. He had to remind himself that he and Kage had been taken against their will and, despite outward appearances, Ancula was not to be trusted or sympathized with.

18

"How did we get stuck with the shit detail?"

"You have only been here fifteen minutes and you are already complaining," Lucky said.

"I feel like I have a lot to complain about," Jason said.

They were in a secure location aboard the *Unjuss*, planning out their operation. Both Lucky and 701 had scanned to identify all of the monitoring devices and neutralize them temporarily. There had been surprisingly few.

"I had the situation well in hand before you arrived," Lucky countered.

"What was your master plan? Let Kage die of old age, and then jump out the airlock? You guys have been on this ship for months."

"This is not an effective use of what little time we have," 701 said. "They will know the monitoring devices are being jammed soon enough."

"What's the story with this guy?" Jason asked. "Is he just stupid, or is it something else? That stunt leaving us on the surface could have got a lot more mercs dead. As it is he'll have to explain the eleven deaths to the guilds."

"He is inexperienced," Lucky said. "While he is a criminal, these sorts of operations are not what he specializes in. He relied heavily on Suta—Poo2—to advise him."

"You said relied...as in past tense," Jason said.

"Suta has fallen out of favor. Right now, I am filling his old role. It is why I was able to get the pair of you over here for this mission."

"How protected is this person?"

"Reasonably so, but not so much as to indicate they are expecting any sort of attack," Lucky said. "The compound was built for luxury not to be impregnable. There are multiple avenues of ingress and egress that will maximize our chances for getting the target out unharmed."

"I am not overly enthusiastic that we are to kidnap an innocent civilian," 701 said.

"Me either," Jason said. "You're certain drugging her is our best option?"

"Vissalo are a strong species," Lucky said. "She would be far more manageable and less prone to self-injury if she was unconscious."

"Your show," Jason said. "Just tell me what you need from me."

The remainder of the time they had left was spent going over the detailed information on the compound that Ancula had provided and trying to plan for any contingencies. The plan that emerged was easily executed by the trio. Jason still had concerns that they wouldn't be able to guarantee the safety of the principle, but Lucky assured him he had that covered.

By the time one of Ancula's security specialists arrived to check on why all the monitoring devices had failed, they were already done with their planning session. It wrapped up quickly enough that Jason had a few more minutes to berate Lucky for getting sucked into Ancula's trap in the first place.

"Are we staying here or going back to the transport?" Jason asked.

"You will remain aboard this ship as guests until this ancillary mission is completed," Lucky said. "Your pay will reflect the guild-required bonus for the change in scope."

"That's what I wanted to hear," Jason said, his voice modulated by his helmet he'd shoved back on before the specialist arrived. "Lead the way to our accommodations."

"Did you guys do anything to any of the equipment in here?" an orderly asked. Lucky turned to face the crewman.

"All we used was the holo-table display," he said. "As far as I know, it is still functioning. What equipment specifically are you referring to?"

"Nothing. Never mind."

"This way," Lucky said, leading them out of the secure area and down toward crew berthing. "You are not being kept under lock or guard, but the ship's internal sensors will be monitoring your location at all times. You are expected to behave accordingly."

"I'm here to get paid not trash someone's ship for the fun of it," Jason said. They were playing it up for the security footage that would almost certainly be pulled and reviewed by Ancula. They needed to keep up the appearance that they had never met and that the mercs were only there for the money.

"Hardly discreet," Jason said as he looked at the shuttle they'd be riding down to the planet's surface.

"It is what is available that can remain anonymous," Lucky said.

The shuttle was a high-end luxury transport from Aracoria. It would definitely draw attention wherever they landed, but the rest of the shuttles aboard the ship could all be identified and tied back to Ancula, which was something they were trying to avoid.

"Armament?"

"Aboard the shuttle," a voice said from behind them. Jason turned and saw Ancula walking up to them. The synth Lucky had called Suta walked beside him and looked at them with naked hostility.

"You're the big boss?" Jason asked.

"I'm the one paying you for this job, yes," Ancula said before turning to Lucky. "Change of plans. Suta will accompany you down."

"That is not advisable," Lucky said. "We already have our mission and roles planned out."

"Not a request, I'm afraid," Ancula said. "It occurred to me that this is a critical juncture in our operation to not have someone I trust implicitly on-site. You have shown yourself willing to honor our agreement, but that is not the same as being loyal. Suta goes along."

"If I catch even a hint of betrayal, I will kill all of you," Suta said, staring at Lucky.

"I am here to do a job," 701 said to Ancula. "That does not include being insulted by this...abomination."

"Suta, manners," Ancula said. "In and out, Lucky. Quick and clean."

"Do not worry," Lucky said. "We are prepared."

"Then, go. Get it done."

They all boarded the shuttle as Ancula walked away. He reminded Jason so much of Bondrass that his skin crawled. Vissalo weren't all that common in the quadrant and, oddly enough, every single one he had met had been connected to organized crime in some way or another.

Before the hatch had even closed, Jason went over and opened the crates sitting on the deck, pawing through the assortment of weapons and snorting in disgust at what was available. It was just a couple plasma carbines and a small selection of sidearms. Given his lack of options, Jason hoped they were flying toward a soft target.

"This job would be easier without the squish," Suta said, using the common synth slur for biotics.

"But far easier yet without you," 701 said.

"Have we met before?" Suta asked. "I have met almost every battlesynth ever built, yet you are completely unfamiliar to me."

"I am not surprised. A standard synth of your age would certainly have begun to display signs of matrix instability and cognitive decline," 701 said.

"This is Combat Unit 302," Lucky said. "And let us try to remain professional and focused on the task at hand."

Suta fell silent but continued to glare at 701. Jason knew that 701 genuinely despised him, but that wasn't why he was antagonizing the franken-synth. If Suta was focused on him, he wouldn't be digging into who Jason really was. If they had been tracking Lucky for as long as they claimed, it was reasonable to assume they would have information on who he had been flying with all these years.

The shuttle zipped through the atmosphere of the planet with barely a whine inside the cabin. Jason was still pretending he had no idea what planet they were over. Ancula had been adamant that they be kept in the dark about details that didn't matter for the job, but Lucky had told them it was a world called Arospor-4.

"Four-point-two-seven minutes," the announcement came from the flightdeck over the speakers, Jason's neural implant converting the unit of measure into an awkward decimal number. He accessed a top-level menu for the device and made sure his settings hadn't changed. Jason still used seconds, minutes, and hours when discussing time, but he'd adapted his thinking so that he was referring to Jenovian Standard Time. For some reason, it was converting back to Earth Time. If this wasn't a one-time glitch, it was going to get annoying on an op that relied on timing.

"What is the plan?" Suta asked.

"You stay the hell out of our way while we recover the target," Jason said. "We come back to the shuttle, fly back to the ship, and you stay the hell out of our way some more."

"Such a clever little squish." Suta sneered. Jason flipped him off, even though he knew the synth would have no idea what it meant. Still felt good.

"Landing," the pilot announced. The shuttle was so smooth there was no bumping or jostling. The hatch slid open, and Jason could see the aircraft they'd procured sitting across from them on the ramp. He grabbed the weapons he wanted and hopped out.

"Where do you think you are going?" Suta asked.

"This is going to be a long mission if you keep asking moronic questions. Obviously, I'm going to the aircraft, which is a part of our mission profile. You'd know that if you weren't just some tourist tagging along behind us."

"I will fly," Suta declared.

"David Byrne is flying the aircraft," Lucky said. "You will not interfere. You are here as an observer."

"So, you think," Suta said darkly.

"What the fuck does that mean?" Jason asked, turning around to face him.

"Maybe I'm here because Ancula suspects you're not really cooperating as much as you seem to be," Suta said, speaking to Lucky. "Maybe he sent me to—"

"If you interfere with my mission or cause harm to the target, I will do what I should have done on Pyriat-2 all those years ago and rip you apart, piece by piece," Lucky said, stepping in close and deploying his arm cannons. "Your choice."

"We're wasting time," the other synth said, backing down and walking away. Lucky watched him for a long moment before retracting his weapons and following.

"See?" Jason said to 701. "I told you this would be fun."

19

"The squish has some piloting skills, at least."

Jason kept the craft low and slow, blending in with the randomly dispersed air traffic and working his way in toward the target compound, spiraling inward as he dipped in and out of sensor coverage.

"We'll be landing in a few minutes," he said, ignoring the annoying synth.

The property where they were landing the aircraft had a certified landing pad so they wouldn't be attracting any attention from the local authorities. During the initial mission planning, Lucky had found it and reached out to the group that owned it. He discovered it was a small commercial space and that it was currently unused. Posing as a potential buyer, he secured permission to use the landing pad. By the time the property broker discovered they never even bothered to look around, they'd be long gone.

"We were never pinged by anything other than the automated traffic control system. I think we're good."

"He stays here with the aircraft?" Suta asked.

"We need him. He's coming with us," Lucky said.

"What about our egress?"

"If you're scared, you can stay here," Jason said, grabbing his gear and hopping out of the vehicle.

What the synth didn't know was that the plan called for them to steal one of the compound's ground vehicles to make their escape. The problem with trying to use the aircraft for a pickup was that it was clearly the first thing the enemy expected as the property had a sophisticated, powerful anti-aircraft weapon emplacement. When Jason saw the intel imagery, he couldn't believe they were able to legally put something like that in such a densely populated area. It had enough juice to shoot down pretty much anything smaller than the *Phoenix*.

"We are early," 701 said.

"We can walk slowly so we get there on time," Jason said. "Let's move."

They made it to the street over from the compound, but Jason could see the imposing walls from where they stood. The light of late evening was fading as Lucky pulled three tubes from a pack he carried and began setting them up on the ground. They were nestled between two smaller buildings that looked like they could be either storage or utilities.

"What are those?" Suta demanded.

"Shut up, asshole," Jason said as Lucky finished aligning the tubes on the baseplate, angling them toward the compound.

"One more word, Squish..." Suta lifted his left arm and aimed his cannons at Jason's face.

"These are ready," Lucky said. "Time to reposition."

The group retreated back two streets, and then moved up three blocks before approaching the compound again from the side. There was a heavy alloy security door in the wall with no handles or locking mechanisms on the outside. It was actually below the ground level of the compound and looked like it could stop a hit from an anti-ship cannon.

"Ready when you are," Jason said. Both battlesynths switched over to combat mode with a double *pop/whine*. Suta did something similar, but the effect was far less impressive. There was a harsh hissing sound, and the smell of ozone as the prototype weapon systems, now well past their intended lifespan, fully powered up. Instead of the usual glowing red of battlesynth multi-spectrum eyes, some sort of auxiliary optics deployed and covered Suta's eyes.

It took several seconds for Suta to arrive at full-combat mode and, once he did, Jason had to admit the creature was intimidating, but not in the way a real battlesynth was. There were tremors that shook his limbs as his overtaxed power system tried to smooth things out, and the morphic-metal skin of his face was fixed with a strange, manic expression.

"Launching," Lucky said, firing his repulsors and rocketing off into the sky, heading away from the compound.

"What's the plan? What's the plan? What's the plan?" Suta chanted, bouncing from one foot to the other. 701 looked at Jason and just shook his head.

A moment later, there were nine distinct *foomps* as the mortar tubes, each disposable tube loaded with three independent mortars, fired and arced away toward the main gate of the compound. These were medium-yield warheads, but nine hitting in quick succession mangled the heavy, solid alloy gate, as well as the supporting structures around it. Alarms blared, and there were screams behind the walls when Lucky rocketed overhead, disappearing over the wall.

"Launching," 701 said, firing his repulsors and arcing up and over the wall. Unlike Lucky, he didn't have a sustained flight mode, but he had plenty of lift capacity to get him over.

"I'll cover the front," Suta said, taking off at a sprint back toward the main gate.

"What? No! Fuck... Suta just took off," Jason said into the com.

"Took off to where?" Lucky asked.

"Main gate," Jason said. "He got real twitchy right before the mortars fired."

"No change to the plan," 701 said. "Ignore him for the time being."

"I'm ready out here," Jason said.

Lucky shot across the open ground of the compound and right through a window on the third floor. He cut his repulsors and slid across the expensive tile, grabbing at furniture and fixtures to arrest his momentum and, eventually, slammed into a far wall, breaking halfway through into the next room.

He looked up just as an unarmed Vissalo ran into the room so he shot him with a stunner blast, putting him down. Lucky sprang to his feet and ran out of the room and to the right. He had less than half a minute before troopers would arrive to secure the objective and get her to a bunker. If that happened, there would be no way to recover her.

"I am inside," he reported. "No resistance."

"Executing," 701 reported. The battlesynth was the second diversion, opening fire on the outside of the main building to try and draw as many armed guards away from the top floor as possible.

"Charges planted," Jason said. "This feels like overkill."

"It is," Lucky confirmed. "Detonate."

"Fire in the hole."

The building shook from a massive explosion from just outside the wall. Jason had just breached the security door that led down into the tunnels below the compound, which would further confuse the guards trying to coordinate a defense. With luck, they would be forced to split their attention between two breaches, unsure which one was the real assault and which was the diversion.

"I'm clear," Jason said. "Pulling back to position Charlie."

"Copy," Lucky said. "Approaching the target now."

Lucky approached the VIP suites at a full run, opening fire on the armed guards who looked confused and scared. They were wearing discreet body armor so, unfortunately, deadly force was needed. Ancula had asked him to keep it at a minimum, only killing when necessary, which suited Lucky's sensibilities just fine.

He stopped before the large double doors, listening for a moment before kicking them in. A young Vissalo female snarled and fired a weapon at him. He raised an arm to protect his eyes, but the plasma bolt hit him in the side, scorching his armor plating and setting off a series of damage alerts. Lucky dropped and rolled backward as she fired again, this time blasting a hole through the wall. Before she could line up a third shot, he hit her with the tranq pistol he'd been carrying in his left hand. The dart hissed across the room and struck her in the neck. Impressively, she squeezed off one more shot before succumbing to the cocktail of drugs. What wasn't so great was that she lit much of the furniture on fire, setting off the fire suppression system.

Lucky pulled a custom-made bag from his pack and quickly put the Vissalo female into it. The bag would protect against thermal shock, some kinetic impacts with its active armor cells, and dissipate an impressive amount of energy weapons fire. It was a bit of added insurance given how adamant Ancula was she not be harmed.

"Objective secured. Exiting now."

"Sky is clear. I disabled the anti-aircraft batteries on this side," 701 said. "But we have a problem."

"Explain."

"Suta came all the way in through the main gate. He has killed over thirty Vissalo and is now moving into what looks like a barracks."

"I told you he had a twitchy look," Jason said.

"Exfil two. Repeat, exfil two," Lucky said, switching to one of their contingency plans. Exfil two meant everyone pulled back to the aircraft any way they could.

"You want to leave him behind?" 701 asked.

"Ideally, I would like to crush his head with my hands," Lucky said. "We can only hope the Vissalo hit him with something heavy."

Lucky moved without resistance to a door that led out onto a narrow terrace that gave him enough room to get his captive in position across his shoulders and launch. His trajectory and attitude were less than optimal with the addition of the heavy, awkward load, but he managed to fly out over the wall and into the night without anyone taking a shot at him. He risked a look back and saw that the compound yard was strewn with bodies, some dismembered.

So much for minimal killing.

"All this trouble to steal a sack of potatoes?" Jason poked at the bag Lucky carried.

"I almost forgot what it was like working with you," Lucky said as he maneuvered his captive into a seat, opening the bag around her face.

"Are we actually leaving that psychopath synth?" Jason asked.

"Return to the shuttle. The crew there can make the decision of what to do with Suta," Lucky said. "He is not part of my mission objectives."

"Works for me." Jason shrugged. He smoothly brought the aircraft off the ground and shot off into the night, randomizing his course and utilizing the same tricks he had on the way out so they weren't tracked directly back to the shuttle. The ride was quiet save for the snorts and snarls from the heavily sedated Vissalo in the back.

20

"New report just hit the Zadra Network on one of our active queries."

"Regarding?" Twingo asked.

"A compound on Arospor-4 was attacked," Doc said. "Many Vissalo dead and rumors of a missing VIP. The compound was a property held by the controlling family of the Vaiccr Syndicate."

"Why is this interesting?" Crusher asked.

"The assault team was tiny," Doc said. "A battlesynth, a black killbot whose description matches Lucky, and a bipedal being wearing armor. There was also apparently another synth there, but it's only mentioned once."

"Jason and 701 have managed to link up with Lucky, but instead of coming home, they started blowing up gangster hideouts?" Mazer asked.

"Knowing Jason, his brilliant plan was to get himself captured by the same people holding Lucky," Twingo said. "I'm assuming they're now both working to free Kage and escape."

"So, Ancula *is* on a vengeance quest," Morakar said. "We now have a more narrowed focus."

"Maybe, maybe not," Mazer said. "This VIP they kidnapped...that might be leverage. If it was just revenge, why not just wipe the compound out from orbit?"

"We need to find out who Lucky and Jason just kidnapped," Doc said. "Once we have that, we can—" An emergency channel request alert cut him off. Twingo checked who it was from and put it up on the main display.

"Looking around that bridge, I'm assuming you haven't found Jason yet?" Admiral Marcus Webb asked.

"Not much of a greeting, Admiral," Crusher rumbled. Webb looked startled, and then peered closer at the screen.

"Crusher? Have you had some work done?"

"We haven't located him yet," Doc said, redirecting Webb. "I assume this is important?"

"Seeladas Dalton was just assassinated," Webb said. "They were able to capture the assassin...a human."

"It definitely wasn't the captain," Twingo said.

"We know who it was. Carolyn Whitney. The Cridal are holding her, but our relationship with the Cooperative is nonexistent at the moment. Earth voted to leave, and now a human assassin just happens to take out their premier."

"Oof," Mazer grunted. "That's bad."

"Yes, it is," Webb said.

"The reason I'm reaching out is I need to speak to Jason and Abiyah," Webb said. "The Cridal are out for blood. They're sending Red Strike teams out after anyone they deem a *rogue human element*, and that pair would certainly qualify. We've disavowed Whitney, of course, and pointed out she has been off Earth and working as an assassin for nearly a century, but this has now turned political."

"The Cridal aren't going to move militarily against Earth, are they?" Crusher asked.

"Not likely," Webb said. "We've begun talks with the Eshquarian Empire to form a mutual defense pact and, at this point, they fear our navy too much to risk a direct confrontation. But it's still a tense time in the region."

"We'll warn him...if we ever catch up to him," Twingo promised. "He'll be more worried about your scout teams than anything else, if you catch my meaning."

"Unfortunately, I do," Webb said. "But there's little I can do about that. Captain Brown already has orders and is preparing for deployment. Thankfully, he shares his father's absurd level of luck, but he's a little smarter than the old man."

"He'd almost have to be," Crusher grunted.

"Keep me in the loop if you find him," Webb said. "They're going to want to avoid the Lower Orion Region for the time being."

"He'll appreciate the heads up," Doc said. Webb nodded to him and killed the channel.

"This is interesting, but hardly pressing." Crusher shrugged. "If we're having so much trouble finding him, I'm not too worried about a Red Strike team getting there first."

"But Abiyah is on S'Tora still with a bunch of kids," Twingo reminded him.

"Good point," Crusher said. "We're going to need to pick up the pace."

"How in the absolute fuck..."

Jason dropped the aircraft down and set it near the shuttle. It was right where they had left it, but it was on fire, and there were bodies all around it. Suta stood amongst the flames, watching them as Jason landed.

"More Vissalo bodies," Lucky noted.

"The stupid bastard led them right back to the shuttle," Jason said. "While we were dancing around playing games, he came straight back here. Want me to lift off?"

"Stay down, but keep the engine running," Lucky said, opening the door and stepping out.

"Where have you been?" Suta shouted over the noise.

"What have you done, you absolute imbecile?" Lucky asked.

"Everything we did was to make certain Ancula was isolated from the abduction, and you led them right back here."

"You left me behind!" Suta said.

"We had a mission. It did not include allowing you to indulge yourself with unnecessary killing."

"I was helping! I was vital! Without me, you'd have never recovered her."

"Lucky, we're going to need to wrap this up," Jason said. "Authorities are on the way. Is any of the shuttle crew left alive?"

"It does not appear so," Lucky said, pointing to the three bodies wearing the same blue coveralls the rest of Ancula's crew did.

"They came out and aimed their weapons at me," Suta said.

"That crazy bastard murdered his own shuttle crew?" Jason muttered to 701.

"He is unstable and dangerous," 701 said. "This is hardly a surprise."

"Damn," Jason said. "You guys should have killed him years ago."

"Cannot argue with your logic," 701 said.

Jason looked down at his displays and leaned back out the door.

"We need to leave, *now!*" he shouted. "We have less than two minutes to clear the area or we'll be fighting our way out."

Suta shut his weapons down and walked over to the aircraft, climbing into the aft cabin as if nothing had happened. Lucky climbed in on the other side, checked their captive, and then nodded to say that he was ready. Jason slammed the power up on the ascent thrusters and yanked the nose away from the incoming law enforcement and emergency service aircraft. The small craft zipped away from the burning shuttle, Jason having no idea where he was going other than away.

"We need to arrange alternate transportation back to the ship," Lucky said. "Head north toward a city called E'poe-Nami. It is near—"

"I've already got it," Jason said as he punched it into the navigation system. "Standby... I'm climbing up into the normal traffic lanes to hopefully blend in. How's our passenger?"

"Unconscious for at least the next six hours," Lucky said.

"If we can avoid any more killing sprees, we should be there in about two hours," Jason said. "Maybe our luck will hold out until then."

It did not.

They hadn't made it even a quarter of the way to their destination when an alert came up on the navigation panel instructing them to land at a nearby aerodrome or be intercepted. Jason had no idea what they might be intercepted by, but it was a safe bet whatever the locals had was faster than his aircraft...and armed.

"Problem," he said. "We've been spotted, and I have nowhere to run. I don't even know where the hell we're at. Having an abducted and drugged civilian aboard along with a psychotic murder-bot that just left behind two massacres probably won't help our chances when they force me down."

"Is there any way to get in contact with the *Unjuss*?" Lucky asked Suta.

"I have a tracker on me," Suta said quietly. The synth sounded lethargic like it had just come off a bender. "If we can land and hide, they will find us."

"That's hardly reassuring," Jason said. "We probably have about ten minutes before they send interceptors. Where do you want to put down? There's no way in hell we're making it to E'poe-Nami."

"Descend out of the traffic lane and fly west toward that settlement in the distance," Lucky said. "We will ditch at the first available landing site and try to escape and evade."

Jason grunted and pushed the craft into a steep, spiraling dive to shed altitude as quickly as possible. It wasn't a fighter so he couldn't just nose over and come out at the bottom of a high-G pullup without ripping the stubby wings right off. As it was, he had to pay attention to his indicators to make sure he wasn't pushing the flimsy thing past its limits.

701 helped as best he could by ripping the interior panels and insulation down from the roof and yanking the cable out of the dorsal-mounted transponder antenna, making it that much harder to

track them. Jason took a moment to peek over his shoulder and saw that Suta stared out of his window, his face expressionless. He'd been out in space for a long time and stared down some formidable opponents during all that, but he had to admit to himself that the clearly insane synth with weapons bolted to it sitting behind him scared the shit out of him. He kept expecting him to switch back to a manic state and start blowing holes in the aircraft while they were airborne.

"There is an airfield to port," 701 said. "Agricultural service field by the looks of it."

"I got it," Jason said, bearing toward the field as they leveled out.

He pushed the speed as high as he could and still have any hope of slowing to a stop without overshooting the airfield and having to circle back. Thankfully, it was the middle of the night and the facility was abandoned, though brightly lit. He was assuming there would be some sort of security, but not likely armed.

"There is a hangar with the door open," Lucky said.

"They all have their doors open," Jason said. "Actually, I don't think they have doors. Let me see if there's any space to roll this thing out of sight."

He came in hot and landed, the gear slamming into the taxiway as the vertical thrusters howled and sent debris swirling through the air. The hangar to his left had a wide enough space to park in, so he steered into it, moving the small craft as far back from the entrance as he could.

"Shit. You'll still be able to see the tail if you're low enough."

"Unavoidable," Lucky said. "Let's move. There is a ground vehicle outside that we can clear the area in."

"A ground vehicle?" Suta asked. "We have no time for that."

"None of the aircraft here are suitable for our needs," 701 said. "Now, move."

They lifted the snoring Vissalo out of the aircraft and moved quickly to a row of beat-up work vehicles with large wheels and high ground clearance. Jason moved up into the single seat cab while everyone else climbed into the back. Since it was a work vehicle that was used by many, the five-digit access code was helpfully written above the keypad. He punched it in, and then started the small turbine that ran the generators and fed power to the drive motors. A few seconds later, he smoothly pulled out of the yard and was moving down the road.

Thankfully, the road was paved so he wasn't kicking up a visible dust trail as he drove. He kept the lights off and used his helmet's low-light mode to navigate through the dark. He decided to keep heading south and, hopefully, they'd gain enough distance and Ancula would be able to send a shuttle to retrieve them. He shook his head at how screwed up things had gotten because Ancula sent along a homicidal synth that couldn't be controlled.

"Pursuing aircraft are overflying the area now," Lucky reported over the com. Jason couldn't see them, but he imagined he could feel the subtle vibrations from their passing through the floorboards. "They did not slow down over the airfield."

"Maybe they think nobody would be so stupidly obvious as to land at the first airfield they saw," Jason said.

The vehicle they had stolen actually had decent speed, and they were quickly leaving the facility behind. It took a little getting used to since the steering was a knob on the right arm rest with the throttle and brake done by the same lever on the left. He knew once the pursuing aircraft figured out they weren't ahead of them, they would break up and circle back, performing a grid pattern search. It wouldn't be long after that until they found the abandoned aircraft.

"How is she?" he asked.

"Stirring, but still unconscious and stable," Lucky said. "We do not have a lot of time to waste. I did not count on taking this long, and I do not advise giving her a second dose."

"Do you have a second dose?"

"No."

Jason ground his teeth and swallowed down his sarcastic reply. "I'm going as fast as I think is safe. Let's hope Ancula is tracking his pet psychopath and is sending an extraction team."

It was nearly another hour of driving before they had their answer. A shuttle overflew them at high speed and, at first, Jason thought it was one of their pursuers, but once it was past it banked to the left and flared. It set down in a pasture full of some type of large livestock that walked on two hind legs. They looked like a cross between a kangaroo and a buffalo.

"Hang on! It's gonna get bumpy!" He slowed, and then drove the vehicle down through the shallow ditch, up the other side and through the fence. The tall grass had concealed just how rough the terrain was and the vehicle bounced and bucked wildly, threatening to get stuck. Jason applied full power, ignoring the warnings on his display as the drive motors overheated. It laboriously pulled itself out of the swampy ditch and hopped across the field as he tried his best to dodge the animals with limited success.

They slid to a stop behind the shuttle as two of Ancula's blue-uniformed security troopers were waving and screaming something.

"What?" Jason shouted.

"We have inbound! Thirty seconds out!"

"Shit! Lucky! Move your metal asses, we have incoming!"

Lucky leapt from the back of the vehicle cradling his captive while 701 and Suta ran to the shuttle. Jason, using a trick his son had shown him, set his plasma carbine to overload and tossed it into the cab before running to the shuttle himself. He wasn't even all the way up the ramp before he felt it lift and begin accelerating away. One of the crew grabbed him and pulled him aboard as the ramp closed.

"That vehicle just exploded!" someone on the flightdeck shouted.

Jason just slumped into his seat, leaned back, and smiled.

21

"You three...with me."

Lucky, Jason, and 701 trailed behind Ancula through the ship and into the executive suite. No security followed them so, either he was foolishly confident they wouldn't harm him, or there were hidden measures he wasn't seeing. Either way, this didn't feel like his time to strike.

The boss had been there to meet the shuttle and see their captive off to the infirmary. From the look on his face, Jason could tell there was some connection between the two. Suta was sent on some menial task, and Lucky provided Ancula with an initial debrief of the entire debacle right there in the hangar.

"This could not have gone worse," he said once they were all inside the doors closed.

"Perhaps next time let the pros you hired do our jobs and keep your psychotic synth here on the ship," Jason said. "He killed over half the Vissalo in that compound *and* your own shuttle crew. The risk to your captive was exponentially higher than it should have been by sending him along."

"Remove your helmet. I'm not speaking to a face shield," Ancula said. When Jason hesitated, he stepped in close. "I said remove it. Is there a problem."

"It's a matter of environmental factors that—"

"That is not a rebreather helmet. Take it off. Now."

Jason sighed and unlatched the helmet, slipping it off over his head.

"Of course," Ancula said wearily. "Jason Burke... Lucky's companion."

"Now you see why I didn't want to take it off," Jason said. "I wanted it to be a surprise. I had this whole routine planned where I would take all my clothes off except for the helmet, and then—"

"Enough!" Ancula hissed. "How are you even here? How did you find me?"

"Money trail," Jason said, not bothering to lie. "I knew your ship from when you left The Gates, and then went from there. We figured out you were moving vast sums of money behind the scenes and tracked it, figuring you would show up sooner or later. After that, it was just an easy matter of bribing the right guildmaster."

"Impressive, but irrelevant now that I know you're here," Ancula said.

"I just want my crew back," Jason said. "I've no interest in whatever it is you're doing, although I am concerned that you let Suta walk around freely after watching him in action."

"He is none of your concern," Ancula said.

"I believe that it is," Lucky said. "You sent him as a trusted observer, and he slaughtered nearly thirty Vissalo for sport. Given how adamant you were that we minimize collateral damage, I imagine his actions will be something that you will have to answer for. As we were the team that executed the raid, it will be us on that line as well."

"You will soon have bigger concerns," Ancula said. "The main mission you were hired for will be starting soon. You should put your focus there."

"Hired?" Jason snorted.

"I have every intention of paying your wage, Jason Burke. Unless you wish to do this for free?"

"I'm not doing shit until I hear what it is, and probably not even then. I came to get my crew back, not get roped into being a hired gun for a thug like you."

"You were so clever to track me down, yet so ignorant of who and what I actually am," Ancula said. "You will be staying here aboard my ship. I cannot trust you aboard the contracted transport. I have your word you will do nothing foolish? Keep in mind, I still hold Kage captive."

"I won't try and damage your ship or escape, if that's what you're asking," Jason said. "I'd like to see Kage."

"You will be permitted to see him. In fact, Lucky can take you." Ancula turned to 701. "I suppose you're not actually Combat Unit 302, are you?"

"701. I am one of Lucky's lot-mates. I also have had firsthand experience with the synth you have named Suta. You would be wise to toss him out of an airlock and let him burn up in the atmosphere."

"Noted," Ancula said. "Lucky, do you vouch for your friends?"

"I do. No harm will come to the ship or personnel while they are aboard."

"Go see your crewmate. I have much to do."

"Aren't you two just thick as fucking thieves," Jason said once they were alone. "Why the hell should I have bothered coming to get you when it looks like you're willingly helping him?"

"I am working to keep Kage safe," Lucky said. "I am also gaining Ancula's trust to undermine Suta and maximize my opportunities to get free, but his reach is long. A simple escape might not guarantee our freedom. In some cases, this being one of them, an antagonistic approach is counterproductive."

"Whatever," Jason said. "So, what's the plan? We have to go kill a bunch of people for this asshole, and then you think he'll just let us go?"

"Hardly. This isn't a simple assault. We will be executing a multi-subject extraction from a secure location. Likely a prison."

"Seems like he could have just hired anybody for that. What did he need you for?"

"He actually needed Seven. Once they discovered the mimic system had been removed, I had to figure out a new angle to make sure I was useful enough to keep Kage alive."

"Hence why you're trying to take Suta's spot." Jason nodded. "Should be an easy sell now that the psycho just killed three dozen soldiers from what I'm guessing was a competitor's cartel."

"Fair assumption," Lucky said, indicating the hatchway into the infirmary.

"I will wait out here," 701 said.

Jason and Lucky walked in, where Kage was sitting up and talking with one of the med techs.

"Captain? You get yourself captured, too?"

"Yeah, but I did it on purpose so that makes me not as stupid as you two," Jason said. "You doing okay?"

"I wasn't permanently damaged," Kage said. "So, what's the plan?"

"We're working on it," Jason said.

"You got yourself captured without working out the details first? That sounds about right."

"Have you learned anything new or useful?" Lucky asked.

"Nothing. All dead ends from what I was doing before," Kage said. "I think they're going to move me to berthing tomorrow. I'll still be under guard, but at least it's not the brig."

"We just captured a young female Vissalo, and this Ancula character says the main mission is about to begin," Jason said. "If we survive, we should be closer to heading home. I could do with a week or so of lounging on the beach after being in a cramped ship with 701."

"You two still hate each other?" Kage asked.

"Eh...I think there's been some improvement on that, actually,"

Jason said. "We can now at least reasonably tolerate each other. So long as we have a common goal, that is."

"I will try to get you involved in the planning phase of the extraction mission," Lucky said. "Ancula has no experience in this sort of thing, and neither does anyone in his employ. I believe that is why he has Suta with him. Despite his instability, he does have a sound tactician's mind."

"Consider me dubious of that claim," Jason said. "So, what the hell is this guy's deal? And why are you so keen to help him?"

"Ancula is a capo in a Vissalo crime family as we'd assumed, but he was what you would refer to as a white-collar criminal," Lucky said. "He is in charge of laundering, transporting, and sheltering money. I'm not saying he doesn't have enforcers who employ violence, but the majority of his operation is managing a network of currency hackers and affiliated banks."

"We've met some of them," Jason said. "A currency hacker named Abrus gave us the information we needed to find you guys."

"Abrus is still alive?" Kage asked.

"You know him?"

"Obviously. Or I know *of* him. Last I heard, he'd pissed off the wrong people and was on the run."

"Apparently, he found protection under Ancula's organization," Jason said. "It took a steep price for him to sell out."

"That sounds like him," Kage said.

"Lucky, you need to be working on a way to get us out of here *without* getting sucked into Ancula's suicide mission," Jason said. "That crew of mercs he assembled might be competent, but they're not a cohesive unit, and they're pissed enough to just walk or try to kill him if they get the chance for that stupid stunt he pulled leaving us in the desert. He's going to get us all killed. If he wants, we can work with him as advisors, and then go back to Enzola-2 and get a proper PMC that has the equipment and personnel to pull this off."

"It is likely too late for that now that we have captured the Vissalo female," Lucky said. "She is to be used as leverage, if I understand it

After looking like he might object, 701 nodded and moved to the corner where he could watch Jason. Kage pulled as much money as he thought he'd need and tossed the bag to the battlesynth before walking out and shutting the door.

He had already run multiple diagnostic cycles on his neural implants, so he was comfortable that he was one-hundred percent mission capable and that Ancula's people didn't try to put any malware in the buffers. The modern terminal had all of the shops and booths a larger complex would have so he was able to buy an unregistered Nexus node with cash as well as a block of slip-com time.

Like an addict who had been clean for months and had just been handed a hit, Kage's fingers trembled as he tore the fresh node from its packaging and interfaced with it. Even just the familiar handshake protocols tickling his neural implants caused him to let out a sigh, leaning back on the bench. Within minutes, he was already propagating out through the local Nexus and collecting intel, planning his next moves. He was still anxious about Lucky remaining aboard that ship and his inability to contact him through the slip-com array on S'Tora, but having his freedom and a full-bandwidth connection again brightened his spirits considerably.

"Time to get to work."

23

"What the hell is the matter with it now?"

"It's an antique ship running one-off, prototype equipment and an untested engine management system," Twingo snapped from inside a service bay. "There are going to be some issues."

Crusher narrowed his eyes, trying to figure out a way to turn that back around to insult the engineer, but the moment came and went. They had landed on a large moon in the Fruch System for an unscheduled stop when the slip-drive dropped them to a lower stable speed and refused to allow them to increase velocity. Thankfully, they were within range of a suitable world to stop and make repairs.

"Have you guys ever thought of getting a newer ship?" Mazer asked.

"Don't talk to me about that," Twingo said, his voice muffled. "Jason already made it clear if the *Phoenix* was rolling down a hill, he would use our corpses as wheel chocks to stop her. Just to give you an idea of his priorities."

"I like her," Morakar said. "Modern ships lack any artistry or aesthetic. They are all blocky and ugly. The *Phoenix* looks like a predator, as all warships should."

"Is main power back up?" Doc asked.

"I never took it down," Twingo shouted, now deeper into the bay. "Where the hell did you go?"

"I arranged for fuel and provisioning like you asked," Doc said. "You talk to the Eshquarians yet?"

At this, there was the sound of slamming tools and an uninterrupted string of cursing as Twingo wriggled his way back out of the service bay and onto the stand, glaring down at his crewmates.

"When the hell would I have time to do that?!" he screamed. "I've been trying to fix the damn ship while this moron keeps asking me stupid questions...because that's what morons do!"

"That's not all we do." Crusher snarled. "Sometimes, we get bored and murder our friends with our bare hands."

"So...was that a yes or no? Did you contact the Eshquarians or not?" Doc asked, barely dodging a panel wrench that Twingo hurled at him.

"That's probably a no," Morakar said.

"Thanks. I picked up on that," Doc said. "I'll handle it."

"What Eshquarian is he talking about?" Mazer asked.

"Hmm?" Crusher asked, pretending he hadn't heard him.

"The Eshquarians," Mazer said.

"What Eshquarians?"

"The ones Doc is going to contact."

"I'm not sure what you're—"

"I'm going to shoot him," Mazer said to his brother.

"Just tell them, Crusher," Twingo said from back inside the service bay. "They won't stop until— Ha! Got you now you miserable bastard!" There was a loud *pop* from inside the bay, and a squeal of pain from the engineer as a wisp of smoke threaded out from the access panel and into the cool evening air. They all stared at the opening for a moment.

"He's fine," Crusher said. "Why do you want to know who Doc is contacting?"

"Because your crew always seems to have the inside line on things, even before Galvetic Intelligence catches wind of it," Mazer said. "I want to know what new connection you might be exploiting."

"The captain has a...personal relationship, I guess you'd say, with the new Minister of Imperial Intelligence," Crusher said. "We're hoping they will still work with us since Jason is currently otherwise engaged."

"You think Jason hasn't already contacted them?" Morakar asked.

"Maybe," Crusher said. "But he might not know what we know, so he wouldn't know what to ask, and we have no idea how long the SX-5 has been sitting on Enzola-2. He might not even have access to slip-com right now."

"What are you hoping to learn?"

"We've put together a solid but limited dossier on Ancula. We're hoping the Eshquarians can fill in the details. The Vaiccr Syndicate operates well outside of their territory, but this new head of intelligence likes to keep tabs on everything."

"They're one of the bigger operations in this part of the quadrant," Morakar said. "Maybe we'll get lucky."

———

"Dr. Ma'Fredich. How good it is to see you."

"Similan," Doc said, giving T'Cali Amon's trusted right hand a genuine smile. While he loved his crewmates like family, it was nice to interact with someone with proper manners and social etiquette once in a while. "I trust you are well?"

"Well enough," Similan said. He was at one time the consigliere to the most powerful crime lord in the quadrant: Saditava Mok of the Blazing Sun Syndicate. Now that Mok had resumed his true identity and been named as the head of Imperial Intelligence, Similan had continued his service as T'Cali Amon's chief of staff. "While I enjoy our talks, you have the air of someone in distress."

"Indeed," Doc said. "Have you had any recent contact from Jason Burke?"

"We have not. Is he not with you?"

"No. He and one of the battlesynths of Lot 700 took off after Lucky and Kage. We're trying to track their movements, but the trail is growing cold, and now we're hoping to get ahead of them, hence why I'm contacting you. I realize that your obligations to the Empire mean that you might not be in a position to help, but I have to ask anyway."

"Understandable," Similan said. "And you're correct, using imperial resources to help you out would be...problematic. There are controls and protocols in place that we must at least pretend to honor."

"I understand. We'll try and—"

"I did not say we wouldn't help," Similan held up a hand. "Only that you might not like the terms."

"Go on."

"If Omega Force was listed as an outside contractor or an available asset, it would make it far easier for us to provide what intel we might have."

"I would need to see the details of such an arrangement," Doc said. "If I entered us into a binding agreement with Amon, even with him and Jason getting along the way they seem to now, Jason would probably still twist my head off out of general principle."

"I always appreciated the captain's direct leadership style," Similan said. "Perhaps if it was arranged through a third party?"

"We have a few dummy corporations we work through that will pass inspection if you're audited," Doc said. "Perhaps the agreement can be with one of those."

"This could be workable. Please, send me what you have and what you need, and I will see if we can reach an acceptable arrangement," Similan said. "Understand that such an agreement would not open the door to unlimited access, of course. This would be something I will push Minister Amon on because it involves recovering Lucky."

"And Kage," Doc reminded him.

"He will not care about that," Similan said. "Kage annoys him."

"Yeah...we hear that a lot."

"Forward your information, and I will prioritize it."

Similan killed the slip-com channel on his end, and the display winked out. Doc quickly bundled the data they'd collected from the Zadra Network and other various sources and transmitted it to Eshquaria. It was a few moments later that everything went dark and silent save for the faint sound of Twingo cursing at the top of his lungs at the aft end of the ship.

"I'm going to kill that rat bastard."

Jason woke up with a splitting headache and sore muscles, his brain trying to kick into gear and piece together what happened. The stunner shot had sufficient power to overcome his enhancements and the armor's ability to shunt the energy so it packed quite a punch.

"He did no differently than you would have if you were in his position," 701 said.

"I'm guessing you volunteered to stay since he couldn't stun you," Jason said. "Is Kage okay?"

"He is fine. He is working to arrange transportation for us."

"Still can't get a hold of anyone back home?" Jason frowned.

"The com array at your base is non-responsive," 701 said.

"That's...concerning," Jason said. "Twingo gets absorbed into what he's doing on these major overhauls, but Doc at least should have known the array was down and reset it. Any contact with your buddies?"

"No. But nor is there a general distress issued letting me know that something has happened."

"Weird," Jason said.

"What's weird?" Kage asked as he walked in.

"Still can't get a hold of any of the others."

"I'm mildly worried about that," Kage said. "Maybe there was an accident with the rebuild, and Twingo managed to blow up the entire—"

"Stop!" Jason said, rubbing his head. "Unhelpful. What have you been up to that is of use in our current situation?"

"I found us a ship."

"What kind of ship."

"A spaceship."

"Kage..."

"Look, it's just sitting there. All alone. Nobody has come to check on it for months and months. It's lonely."

"We are not stealing someone else's ship," 701 declared.

"Well," Jason said, "let's not take that completely off the table just yet. Our options are a little thin at the moment."

"You are seriously considering this?" 701 asked.

"Kage, details," Jason said, holding up a hand to cut the battlesynth off from further comment.

"It's an executive transport. High speed, light armor, and minimal defensive weaponry. It's owned by a shell corporation that's actually rumored to be connected to the Vaiccr Syndicate in some way, but its registration is clean. It's sitting fueled and ready to go."

"Comments?" Jason asked 701.

"The ship technically belongs to a criminal element currently holding one of our friends captive. I see no issue in borrowing it for a time."

"I knew you could be reasonable," Kage said. "It's parked in a private section of the starport, but I've got a way in."

"Let's get moving," Jason said, swaying a bit as he stood up. "Hopefully, it's provisioned. I'm starving."

Instead of leaving the main terminal, Kage led them back through a secure door he'd already hacked into and into the maintenance areas. They passed a handful of workers but walked by them with confidence and purpose. Most ignored them, one turned to gape at the battlesynth but otherwise showed little interest in what they were doing there. Since it was a secure area, and they appeared to know where they were going, everyone just assumed they belonged there.

"Standby," Kage said. "I need to get into this door."

As Kage initiated a connection with the encrypted locking mechanism, Jason looked at the placard next to the door.

Lower-level access. Authorized personnel only.

"Got it," Kage said quietly, pulling the door open a crack.

"That was fast," Jason said.

"This is just meant to keep out casual trespassers and nosy employees," Kage said. "Not determined master criminals like us."

The stairs went down much farther than Jason would have guessed until they found themselves in an impressively large, arched tunnel. It was big enough to move heavy equipment around through, and even smaller ships like his own SX-5 if the wings were folded up in a stowed configuration.

"What the hell is all this?" he asked.

"This starport used to be a military base. These tunnels were used to move munitions to different parts of the airfield without being spotted from orbit or risking an airstrike," Kage said. "This will go all the way to a depot in the direction we want to go, and then a smaller one leads underneath to the secure section we need to get into."

"What do they use it for now?" 701 asked.

"Mostly storage," Kage said. "Up ahead, there are rows of lockable cages built into the walls for spare parts used by the starports maintenance and service companies."

They continued on, passing the occasional port worker or automated vehicle tasked with pulling parts kits and being ignored by both. It was nearly two klicks before the tunnel opened up into an impressively large dome that served as a hub for other tunnels coming into it. It was currently being used as a storage area for specialized flightline equipment like reactor service vehicles and slip-drive alignment trailers.

"We go down that smaller one," Kage said, pointing to their left. "I have to take care of something when we get to the opening to make sure the passive security sensors in the tunnel don't trigger an alert."

"How the hell do you know so much about their security systems and tunnel layouts?" Jason asked.

"You were knocked out for hours. That's more than enough time for me to dig into their network and pull out everything I need to know." Kage sniffed.

"How will you spoof the passive sensors?" 701 asked.

"Don't have the time or equipment for that," Kage said. "I'm going brute force intrusion and shutting them down completely. They won't figure out the system is down until their next maintenance cycle, which is hopefully not for at least a day."

The panel Kage needed was unlabeled and next to an electrical distribution panel. 701 forced the cover off, and Kage quickly went to work silencing the alarm from the panel being accessed. Once he did that, he extended two pairs of nanite tendrils and interfaced directly with the panel. It was something Jason knew he didn't like doing because of the risk factor from being hooked in directly, but none of his equipment had been given back to him before they'd been tossed off the ship.

"You know, I just realized this is all pretty much your fault," Jason said.

"I can't want to hear this," Kage muttered.

"If you hadn't gotten shot back on that platform, we wouldn't be stuck down here right now."

"Actually...you might have a point."

"I do not understand," 701 said.

"Lucky was captured by Ancula while looking for medical care for Kage," Jason said. "He'd been shot during a mission on a platform call The Gates, and Ancula offered to patch him up in return for a favor. You didn't know that?"

"I only knew the pair had been captured," 701 said. "I had assumed Kage was injured in the process of that, which was how they were able to capture Lucky as well."

"That would have been a cooler story," Kage said, his eyes narrowed as he worked through the layers of digital security.

"You going to take all damn day at this?" Jason asked.

"Funny," Kage said. "You have no idea how relaxing it was being held captive by a ruthless gangster if for no other reason to escape this constant abuse. There...that's probably it."

"Probably?"

"We'll know pretty soon after walking down the tunnel." Kage shrugged. "You can have it done quickly, or you can have it done right...not both. I also disabled all the door sensors and locks, so we won't be wasting time ripping them down."

"Or leaving evidence we came this way," Jason said. "Fine. Put the panel cover back on, and let's get going."

24

"The transition is a lot smoother."

"The starboard proportional valve was lagging behind its counterpart," Twingo said. "They have to match position within a tolerance of plus or minus point-zero-zero-two. To stay matched, the portside valve had to open and close slower than it likes, which caused it to flutter. That was the jolt you were feeling during transition."

"If you nerds are done fluttering your valves, where are we going?" Crusher asked.

"Your least favorite place in the galaxy," Doc said.

"Your house?"

"No, you moron. Colton Hub," Doc said. "And what the hell is wrong with my house?"

"Other than the gross specimen jars on shelves and the boring music playing? Nothing," Crusher said. "What's on the Hub?"

"We got a contact from Similan that might have information on this Ancula," Doc said. "Turns out this guy has popped up seemingly out of nowhere fairly recently, and they've not developed a full background on him yet. They're giving us the intel they have with the agreement we'll look into it and give them whatever we find in return."

"Colton Hub is quickly becoming almost civilized," Mazer said. "Once they opened up the Yarret Expanse to colonization, most of the convoys ran through the Hub. Only took a few high-profile incidents for the corporations to come in and start cleaning the place up."

"Hopefully, that means literally cleaned up as well," Twingo said. "The place was disgusting. The lower decks? Nightmare fuel."

"How's the slip-drive look?" Doc asked.

"You're good to go," Twingo said. "She'll run all the way up to ninety percent slip without any trouble now."

"Let's see about that," Doc said, slapping the control on his left to engage the drive. The *Phoenix* surged to her desired velocity and meshed-out with barely a ripple of dissipating slip energies to mark her passing.

———

"Wow. They really have cleaned up on here."

"Not too bad at all," Crusher remarked, sniffing experimentally.

"You see all those long-haul heavies on the upper docking arms?" Mazer asked. "They're moving a *lot* of colonists through here. Where the hell are they all going?"

"People are catching on that the ConFed is really gone," Doc said. "A lot of them are scared. For millennia, the fleet was the only thing keeping the strong from preying on the weak in many parts of the galaxy. With that gone, people on worlds at risk from war or invasion are taking their families and leaving."

"Only to be preyed upon by the scum on the fringes of the frontier regions," Morakar said sadly.

"Sometimes, the devil you know isn't the better option," Crusher said. "Think of how many genocides and exterminations the ConFed kept from happening that will now kick off. A lot of these people had no better choice."

"Didn't take you for someone to get all weepy about the fall of the ConFed," Twingo said.

"I hate any authoritarian form of government no matter how benevolent it claims to be," Crusher said. "But I also understand that these are complicated, nuanced arguments. Just because predation of the weak by the strong is bad doesn't mean the ConFed is automatically good because it stopped it and vice versa."

Mazer just stared at him for a moment before turning to Doc. "Did you improve his brain as well when you juiced him?"

"Crusher isn't stupid. He's lazy," Morakar said. "He learned pretty early that if he pretended to be hopelessly incompetent at certain things he didn't like, people would stop asking him to do them."

"You've always understood me," Crusher agreed.

Twingo and Morakar stayed behind to supervise the servicing of the *Phoenix* and watch over her while the others moved out of the hangar bay and into the main promenade. Doc took it all in, eyes wide and mouth hanging open.

It was breathtaking.

The drab, dirty military-turned-industrial look of the promenade had been completely stripped away, and in its place was a bright, colorful, vibrant scene. They'd even installed sky panels in the ceiling that displayed a bright blue sky with wispy clouds blowing across to give the impression of an outdoor bazaar.

"I'm trying to look past the new façade and see the old Hub ugly, but I don't recognize most of these shops, and this is the same hangar complex we always use," Crusher said. "Amazing."

"Look at all the colonists walking around," Mazer said. "They look like they're on holiday. Normally, in this place, they'd all have a furtive, hunted look."

"Because they usually *were* being hunted," Doc said. "I see armed security everywhere. Look like real pros, too."

"Corporate soldiers." Crusher nodded. "Whoever sunk the money into cleaning this place up is making sure it stays cleaned up."

"Shit. Is our guy still going to be here and active?" Mazer asked.

"If Similan gave me his info, he'll be here," Doc said.

They moved through the main section of the promenade, around into A-Quad of the main loop. This section was mostly taken up by government offices with long lines of bored and frustrated-looking aliens trying to get their immigration documents straightened out before boarding ships for their final destinations. Halfway through A-Quad, Doc turned left into a large, arching passage labeled as Zinta Spoke Seven. It was one of the fourteen *spokes* that passed through all the rings, ending at the station's core.

When Colton Hub had been purely a refueling and repair station for deep-space freighters, back before starships had the legs to make it across the quadrant without frequent stops, the ring-and-spoke layout had been an efficient way to move massive parts to and from the docking arms to repair depots near the core. During the Hub's long phase as a lawless haven for smugglers, mercs, and pirates, the spokes had been gauntlets of local thugs preying on tran-sients. Doc had been a part of more than one shootout in these passages.

Now, in the Hub's new iteration as a legitimate center of commerce, the spokes were clean and brightly lit. Business owners who couldn't afford a storefront in any of the three promenades brought carts to line the bulkheads, shouting at passersby that they simply cannot live without whatever the hell it was they were selling.

"Is this where he's at? He has a cart selling intel?" Crusher asked.

"You're a dumbass," Mazer said. "If he's selling intel, he won't just come out and say he's selling intel. He's probably that guy over there selling those cooked rodents."

"How can you tell?"

"If I was selling intel, the perfect cover would be cooked rodents. Think about it. If anybody actually came up to your cart, you *know* they're not there for a charred rodent, because who the fuck wants one of those, right? So, whoever approaches you would have to be someone buying intel. You'd know, they'd know, but station security would just think you're some gross asshole cooking and selling things you caught in the gray water bilge."

"What do you think, Doc?"

"I think I'm having a stroke listening to you two," Doc said. "I'm also pretty sure he's not the rodent salesman."

"That's what he *wants* you to think," Mazer said.

Doc tuned them out as they argued over which vendor could be a secret spy and led them inward until they reached the intermediate ring. This was private offices and residential spaces, so it was much quieter than the frenetic energy of the outer ring. He walked up to the secure entrance of a residential block and activated the call panel.

"Please, state purpose," it said.

"Package drop off," Doc answered.

"Please, state unit or resident."

"Unit I-A-three-two-eight."

"Standby...please, present package."

Doc held up an envelope that contained a datacard.

"Accepted. Please, place package in receptacle," the panel said, and a shallow drawer extended out from underneath the panel. Doc dropped the envelope in and waited as it retracted.

"Thank you. Enjoy your day."

"Now what?" Mazer whispered.

"Now, we go back to the ship," Doc said. "He'll contact us. All the information he needs is on there."

"You ever tried a cooked bilge rat?" Crusher asked Mazer as they retraced their steps.

"No, why would I want to?"

"How do you know it's not amazing? Maybe we're missing out. They could be great and so many people will never know."

"You want me to buy you a cooked rat?" Mazer asked.

"I'll eat one if you eat one."

"Let's just say we both ate one already and make Morakar eat one."

"I like it."

"That was delicious. Thank you."

.   .   .

"We knew you'd like it," Mazer said to his brother with a perfectly straight face.

"Other than dealing with these two, how did it go?" Twingo asked.

"Just a dead drop. Hardly anything to get excited about," Doc said. "Not sure how long it will take until they make contact, but I'd suggest we stay on the ship. He knows we're here."

"We're fully serviced and provisioned," Twingo said. "We can leave as soon as we get a destination. She's going through a little more fuel than I anticipated with the new engines, but there's still a lot of tuning to do."

"How much food did we take on given we're feeding three Galvetic warriors?"

"Should be plenty. Thankfully, I had just had the galley stocked before we had to flee S'Tora."

"How long are we going to wait for this clown?" Crusher asked.

"The clown is already here," a voice said.

"Son of a..." Crusher jumped up and spun around in time to see an alien with pale green skin walk out of the darkened corridor that led to the cargo hold. "Who the hell are you?"

"I thought I made it clear," the alien said. "Which of you is in charge? It certainly can't be this one."

"I-I guess I am?" Doc asked looking around.

"Ah, yes. You most definitely have the decisiveness and quick thinking of a leader," the alien deadpanned.

"This guy is a jerk," Crusher grumbled.

"So are you," Twingo pointed out.

"It's funny when I do it."

"I was asked to come here as a favor to Similan. Am I wasting my time?"

"How about you properly introduce yourself without all the clever commentary and explain how you boarded this ship in the first place?" Morakar suggested.

"Fair enough. Sometimes, I can't help myself. My name is Zem'ulan'ta—"

"I'm not saying that," Crusher said.

"Zem is fine. I'm an intelligence asset for the Eshquarian Empire, no longer a freelancer thanks to Minister Amon making me an offer too good to pass up."

"What was the offer?" Morakar asked.

"Work for me exclusively or I'll kill you," Zem said.

"Effective," Doc said.

"How did you get aboard my ship?" Twingo demanded, the tips of his ears turning purple indicating he was just barely holding in his rage.

"You shouldn't leave the ramp lowered in a place like this," Zem said. "Or you should upgrade the security protocols on your pressure doors if you do." Twingo said nothing, instead just storming out toward the cargo hold.

"He'll be fine." Doc waved off the unspoken question. "You have some information for us?"

"Ancula Suman Sclician Naeourami," Zem said. "An interesting case. Very difficult to track down. Ancula is a Vissalo from the M'aqu Family, the minority faction within the Vaiccr Syndicate, the Vaiccr Family being the majority faction. He is known as the syndicate's money man. Some months ago, he sought to coerce an assassin known as Seven to help him get members of his family released from wherever they are being held. Clear so far?"

"Sure," Mazer said.

"There's a problem with this narrative," Zem said. "It appears that Ancula has only existed for the last three years."

"An alias?" Doc asked.

"Ancula was a real person, but we have confirmation he died five years ago. This isn't widely known, not even to his compatriots. The Vissalo who has your friends right now appears to be Ancula, but we know he can't be."

"Then, who the hell is he?" Mazer asked.

"That's the real question, isn't it?" Zem said, smiling and

spreading his hands. "I hit a wall here, so I began working the problem backward. If this isn't the real Ancula, then who are the Vissalo being held captive he wants to free? It's doubtful that it really is a handful of the real Ancula's relatives. I had to dig pretty deep into the Vaiccr hierarchy. The Vissalo crime families have a fetish for capturing and holding families of those they wish to put pressure on. They all seem to do it, the worst was Bondrass, a Vissalo I believe you have—*had*—some familiarity with."

"Yeah, he was a real gem," Doc said sourly. Out of all the Omega Force crew, it was Doc that had had the most exposure to Bondrass and saw just how depraved he was.

"Indeed," Zem said. "I found four groupings of prisoners in Vaiccr territory that met the requirements. Without knowing who Ancula really is, I cannot narrow it down further." He tossed Doc a datacard. "It's all on there."

"We're a lot closer than we were," Doc said. "Our thanks."

"Your thanks are nice, but hardly the price of that data." Zem laughed. "We expect you to repay our generosity by running this down, and then giving a complete and detailed report to the Ministry of Imperial Intelligence."

"Seems fair." Crusher shrugged.

"Exceedingly so," Zem said. "That's all I have for you, I'm afraid, so I will leave you with a message from my employer: Good luck and go get your friends back."

"Tell Minister Amon we'll do our best and report back as soon as we can," Doc said.

Once Zem had left, and they'd calmed Twingo down, they wasted no time putting the *Phoenix* back into space. The data trove that they'd been given was immense, but the *Phoenix*'s new computers, helped along by Voq's adaptive AI routines, made short work of sorting and categorizing it all. Running a centillion calculations per second, the *Phoenix* parsed the data into four ranked groupings and all of the supporting data in an interface they could easily pore over. It did it before the ship was even outside of the Colton Hub Traffic Control Zone.

25

"It smells nice in here. Like a new ship."

"It pretty much is," Kage said.

The trio had made it through the tunnels leading under the secure landing pads with minimal trouble. The ramp leading up out of the sublevels was guarded by two bored and inattentive Vissalo Jason and 701 made short work of, leaving them unconscious and locked in a parts storage container. For some reason, the thought of killing the pair of lackeys didn't sit well with Jason. Maybe he was getting soft in his old age.

"Flight hours are surprisingly low for a ship that is eight years old," 701 said, pointing to the display on the bulkhead that tracked overall hours as well as how many hours the engines had since overhaul, how much slip-space time she had, and total time in space.

"This is someone's personal transport," Jason said. "Someone important. You sure you can—" Before he could finish the thought, the main panel came to life, and the thrum of the pre-start sequence could be felt though the deck.

"You were saying?" Kage asked, slipping into the copilot seat. "You might want to hurry up and finish your preflight. Once the engines come up, the terminal will know someone is jacking their ship."

Jason hopped into the pilot seat and began going through the familiar procedure of pepping the ship for flight. It had an Aracoria-style helm configuration, so getting her ready to fly was mostly muscle memory.

"I'm ready for engine start," Jason said.

"Go for it," Kage said. "We're ready to— Oh, shit. We're busted. Someone is trying to take control with a ground authority override. Standby."

As the code slicer tried to keep the ground controllers from taking control of the ship completely and locking them out, 701 left the flightdeck and walked aft. Jason assumed he was going to secure the external hatches and ignored him.

"Anything I can do?" he asked.

"Just...let me work," Kage grunted. "Tough...without my interface."

Kage could do miraculous things with just his neural implant and hands, but there were limitations with direct connection, and even more so with manual input. He normally had an interface with him, an intermediate device that helped him control the connection and provide a safety buffer for him. Without it, he had to be much more careful as new systems had advanced and aggressive anti-intrusion protocols meant to keep people like him out.

The panel lights winked on and off as the ground control override appeared to be winning the fight before Kage let out a gasp and all the indicators came back up and full control was restored.

"Nice job!" Jason said, bringing the engines online and thrusting the ship off the pad.

"Wasn't me!" Kage said.

"It was me," 701 said, tossing a device with wiring still attached onto the deck. "Ground authority data transceiver."

"Huh," Kage said. "I probably should have thought of that."

"The tactic does not always work. On most ships, if you attempt to remove or bypass the device, it will lock out all systems. I gambled that this being the ship of a criminal, it would be something they might want to deactivate if needed."

"Can we talk about this later?" Jason asked. "We have pursuers. Kage, armament?"

"She's not a warship, but she's not toothless. Twin-cannons on each wing. Fore and aft missile launchers loaded with intermediate anti-ship missiles. We also have Class 3 shielding."

"Not as much as I hoped, but better than nothing," Jason said. "Get to it. I'm going to try and lose them, but they're coming fast."

The computer was able to classify the three inbound craft as they got closer as Aracorian *Nymer* interceptors. They were fast, but lightly armored and armed. More importantly, they were planet-bound aircraft that wouldn't be able to pursue them into orbit, but they couldn't yet climb out without running right into orbital authority patrols.

"What's the plan?" Kage asked.

"Heading for the southern pole. Try to lose them before we get over the ocean."

"They are within our missile range," 701 pointed out.

"Just," Kage said. "We only have two missiles in the aft launchers. I have to let them get closer before shooting."

Apparently, their pursuers didn't feel the same. Alarms blared, and the sensors locked on to two inbound missiles from the lead craft.

"Shit," Jason grunted, yanking the ship to starboard. He was bleeding off precious speed, but he presented the stronger lateral shielding to the incoming missiles rather than risk a hit on the weaker aft shielding over the engines. Class 3 shields weren't great against missiles or projectiles as it was, far more suited for absorbing and deflecting energy weapons.

"No point defense," Kage said. "Brace!"

The first missile sailed by as the countermeasures scrambled its guidance, but the second slammed into the shield. The explosion rocked the ship and overloaded the shield emitters along the starboard side. They blew out in a shower of sparks, and smoke filled the interior as damage control systems went to work suppressing the fire and clearing the air.

"Heading upstairs!" Jason shouted over the alarms. "Can't chance another hit like that. Prep the slip-drive for a low orbit mesh-out."

"What?!"

"You heard me. Get to it."

"I think I'd rather take my chances with the missiles," Kage said, his hands flying over the controls. "Can this thing even take it?"

"Sure," Jason said unconvincingly.

He pulled the ship into a climb, coming onto an orbital insertion vector and pushing the power up. The ship rocketed away from the engagement, gaining speed as she climbed up into the thinner air. The interceptors tried gamely to keep up but, soon, they had to turn back as they reached their maximum service ceiling without regaining weapons range.

"Orbital authority patrol," 701 said. "Two cutting across transfer orbits to intercept."

"Kage?"

"Vector is clear, safeties disengaged. We'll have one short hop to the outer system, then we'll need to reset the drive and hope she's capable of going on from there."

"When?" Jason asked.

"When your indicators go green, hit it."

Jason hit the engage control as soon as the engines greened up. Instead of the expected subsonic whine of slip-drive engines pushing them out of real-space, they heard and felt a harsh *boom*, and alarms blared.

"Slip-drive is... Well, you can probably guess what you just did," Kage accused. "We're down to subluminal drive only, and even that is now degraded to forty-seven percent."

"Aborting orbital climb," Jason said, struggling to keep his emotions in check. He knew the maneuver had been a risky gamble, but he hadn't seen any other option at the time. Now, his number of options just went to zero. The ship was crippled to the point they couldn't get to space and, even if they could, there was nowhere to run or hide. He had no choice but to descend back to the surface where he knew there were at least three interceptors waiting for him.

"We are losing the main drive," 701 said. A moment later, the indicators caught up with whatever the battlesynth had sensed, and Jason watched his power levels begin to drop. Now, there was a very real fear they might just fall from the sky and crash without anybody else taking a shot at them.

"Failsafes?" he asked.

"The usual. Chemical retrorockets that probably actually still work on a ship this new," Kage said. "One single passenger escape pod."

"If this thing tumbles, I want you in that thing and gone," Jason said. "701 can bail out and land himself."

"And you?" Kage asked.

"I get to pay the price for my own decision making," Jason said. "I'll try to put it down easy, but I think we all know how that will go."

"Drive output under twenty percent," 701 reported with the same amount of emotion one would use to talk about the weather.

"Beginning emergency descent," Jason said. "I'll try to save what's left in the engines for the final touchdown. Threats?"

"I can't pick anything out of the clutter from this altitude," Kage said. "This isn't a gunship."

Jason swung them into a wide, spiraling dive. He deployed what little aero-braking was available and throttled the engines back, hoping to save whatever life remained for one hard, final deceleration.

"Deploy emergency landing boosters," Jason said.

"Blowing the hatches," Kage said.

Sixteen hatches flew off the belly of the ship as the explosive bolts blew them clear. The articulated rocket nozzles moved out into the slipstream providing Jason with an additional bit of drag but also induced a wobble as the irregular shapes disrupted the airflow over the hull.

The largest of the rocket nozzles were nearly fifty centimeters in diameter along the centerline of the ship. Others were as small as three centimeters at the wingtips acting as stabilizers. The system contained ninety seconds of fuel and was fully automated. Once triggered, the computer would take control of the vessel and bring it down in the most direct way possible. In theory, it seemed like a great idea. In practice? Well...Jason had never actually seen one work as advertised yet.

"Passing through twenty-thousand meters," Kage said.

"I've got instruments telling me altitude," Jason said. "Keep your eyes on the threat display."

"I am surprised the ships in orbit have not opened fire," 701 said.

"I'm pretty sure they want to take us alive if possible," Jason said. "See who the hell we are."

As the atmosphere became denser, the buffeting and high-pitched shrieking became more pronounced. He watched as they dropped below five thousand meters and realized they were all committed to the ride. If Kage was going to bail in the escape pod, he would have needed to do it before now.

"Interceptors coming our way," Kage said. "Five of them."

"Perfect," Jason muttered, still angry with himself for taking such a huge gamble. Or, more accurately, angry that it didn't work.

As he crossed two-thousand meters, he pulled up and gently fed power to the drive. It shook the ship and made an unhealthy groaning sound from the aft of the ship, but he held and, soon, their rate of descent reduced from a veritable freefall to just above completely suicidal. He was at fifteen percent output and didn't dare push them any harder.

"Fire the landing boosters."

"Firing," Kage said.

Jason had never been aboard a ship using an emergency landing system. He also vowed never to do so again, preferring to jump out and take his chances. The sounds and vibrations were horrendous. He was slammed around in his flight harness so violently that he couldn't focus on his displays or anything outside of the ship. By the time he could make anything out through the forward canopy, he realized they were about to hit the ground. He tensed up just as one last explosive roar came from the engines and a final, spine-crushing jolt as they slammed into a field. The ship, still carrying a healthy amount of forward velocity, bounced back into the air and skipped twice more across the ground before sliding to a stop.

"Fuel leak on multiple rockets," 701 said calmly. "We must exit the ship immediately."

"Take Kage!" Jason croaked, hitting the release for his harness and trying to get his bearings. 701 extricated the unconscious Veran from his seat and walked to the starboard hatch, yanking the yellow and red handle to blow it from the hull. He leapt out with Jason on his heels.

The scene outside was hell. The field they had crashed into was pre-harvest crops that were dry and combustible. Multiple fires were already raging from the ship's rocket engines, and they were stuck in the middle with a stiff breeze feeding the blazes. Jason looked around to get his bearings, and the first pair of interceptors screamed overhead, pulling up and circling around as the others approached from the south.

"Any chance you could get him clear?" Jason asked.

"No," 701 answered. "The distance is too great to cover without being spotted. We should move upwind away from the ship. There is still a danger of the fuel exploding."

They moved away from the ships and the fires as the smaller ships buzzed around overhead, obviously waiting for something. Jason guessed it would be a shuttle full of armed troops that would come swooping in at any minute to collect them.

"We still alive?" Kage groaned, motioning he wanted to be put down.

"For the moment, but that will probably change quickly," Jason said.

"Ship approaching from the east," 701 said.

"That would be our new friends come to capture or kill us," Jason said bitterly.

It was another ten minutes or so before the ship came into view. The Aracorian combat shuttle swung about and came to a low hover half a klick away and stopped before turning and climbing away slowly.

"What the hell?" Jason asked.

"New ship approaching," 701 said. "Something fast."

Before the shuttle could fully clear the area, a brilliant red plasma bolt lanced out of the sky and destroyed it, blowing the front of the ship off completely. The remaining bit of the aft section spiraled into the ground just as the new ship thundered overhead, engaging the interceptors. Jason couldn't believe his eyes as the *Phoenix* pulled into a hard climb, her engines shaking the ground.

The big gunship came around again and took down two of the interceptors with the chin turret and a third with a missile strike. The last two, realizing they were hopelessly outclassed, turned and ran. The *Phoenix* broke off pursuit and moved to a low hover just ahead. The ramp dropped, and Jason recognized Crusher and Mazer Reddix frantically waving them forward.

"You losers need a ride?" Crusher shouted as Jason leapt up onto the ramp.

"Get us out of here!" Jason said, helping Kage into the hold as the ramp closed up and the ship climbed away.

26

"He's stable. Nothing permanent. Just exhaustion from overtaxing himself."

"Keep him sedated for now," Jason said, leaning against the hatchway to the infirmary. "He's been through an ordeal since The Gates."

The *Phoenix* had easily outrun the next wave of pursuers, climbing up into space and meshing-out without any further exchange of weapons fire even with Twingo flying. Jason had come straight to the infirmary with Kage to help Doc get him situated and begin treatment.

"How did you guys know we were there?" Jason asked. "And what the hell are the Reddix brothers doing with you?"

"We had no idea you were there. We'd been on that planet for two days searching based on intel we received from Similan regarding Ancula's associations," Doc said. "We were in orbit thinking about moving on when we heard on the local net that there was a military action in progress regarding a stolen ship and that we should clear the area. On a hunch, we dropped back down to take a closer look and spotted that executive transport spiraling into the field. The long-range optics identified you and Kage when you stepped out. It was an unbelievable stroke of luck more than anything else."

"No doubt," Jason said.

"Mazer and Morakar came at my request to help with Crusher," Doc went on. "They wanted to observe him in person, and then make the determination of how to handle it."

"What did they decide?"

"They're not going to kill him. Other than that? No idea."

"Eh, either way would be fine." Jason shrugged. "So...this intel you got?"

"Similan put us in touch with an asset they had on Colton Hub that had accurate information on the Vissalo crime families in this area," Doc said. "I'll explain it all to you in a bit. The short version is that the person calling himself Ancula is not the real one. The real Ancula died some time ago, and the Eshquarians have proof of that. We're not sure exactly who the imposter is or what he's after."

"Says his family is being held captive by another faction within the Vaiccr Syndicate," Jason said. "He was going to use Seven to help free them, but then decided to keep Lucky once he learned the assassin and its mimic function were long gone. Lucky stayed with him voluntarily in order to secure mine and Kage's release."

"Interesting. That might help narrow down the target," Doc said. "There is something else I need to tell you, but you're not going to like it. At all."

"Go on."

"The S'Toran authorities moved on us. They seized the hangar base, our homes, planetside accounts...all of it. They'd have gotten the *Phoenix*, but Twingo had her at the farm. We barely made it off-world before they tracked us down again."

"Damn," Jason said quietly. "So, what we have left—"

"Is aboard this ship. The companies you had were left untouched thanks to you isolating the corporations, but I wouldn't suggest going back there or trying to contact anybody anytime soon."

"The Archive?" Jason asked, his eyes going wide.

"Safe. Lot 700 left with Voq aboard the *Devil's Fortune* before we left with the *Phoenix*," Doc said. "They've sworn to keep it safe. They're going to remain in space aboard the ship with it for the time being, bouncing around through slip-space."

"That's something at least. It also explains why Kage hasn't been able to get a hold of you guys. He said the entire com array was down."

"Scorched earth protocols," Doc said. "When they rolled in the gates, Twingo initiated a full wipe and physical destruction of all our computer and com equipment. They'll have gotten nothing useable from the raid save for a lot of spare parts that can only be used on one particular Jepsen Aero DL7."

"Well, this sucks," Jason sighed. "I wonder what political winds have shifted that they suddenly decided to give us the boot."

"Hard to say," Doc said. "We just picked up and ran."

"Let's shelve that for the moment. We still have a missing crewman I need to get back, and then we can come up with a plan on what the hell to do. How's the *Phoenix*?"

"A few little snags here and there but, overall, running as Twingo promised. She's very, very fast."

"Reliable?"

"She's very fast."

"Got it. Back to the old days, huh?" Jason said, laughing humorlessly. "You know what I miss? Way back twenty minutes ago when I thought I was rich and had a beach house."

"Sorry to be the bearer of bad news," Doc said.

"Hardly your fault," Jason said. "You guys did good getting everybody off the surface and wiping the servers. We can deal with everything else. We've done it before."

"It's good to have you back, Captain."

"Hey, dickhead...where is Lucky?"

Jason turned slowly to look at Crusher's head sticking in through the hatchway and resisted the urge to put his boot into it. He had to admit the big warrior looked better, however. That manic energy was gone, and he didn't have that homicidal twinkle in his eye.

"That's what I thought you guys were finding out. Didn't you morons go to Colton Hub to try and get a step ahead?"

Crusher's eyes narrowed.

"I'm glad Twingo wrecked your car," he said as his head pulled back out of the hatchway.

"He what?!"

After Jason had showered, rested, and put on some clean clothes that thankfully had been in his quarters still, they all gathered on the bridge to start putting the pieces together.

"We have three likely targets left," Doc said. "The problem is that it isn't enough to know who this Ancula isn't. What we really need to know who he is in order to narrow it down."

"What about this family?" Jason asked.

"None of the intel Zem gave us mentioned anything about a family. At least not as in actual relatives. Not to Ancula, not even to each other," Twingo said.

"We probably should have woken Kage up," Jason said. "He'll have some background I didn't catch. The last two places we were at seem to be the key. We grabbed a younger Vissalo female out of a guarded compound on Arospor-4 and that was in order gain leverage over someone they were picking up on Kliseri-4. We were dumped out before we could see who."

"The female was most likely Jita Azen-Jer," Twingo said as he punched in the new search parameters. "She's unimportant in the syndicate hierarchy, but she is the sister of a Vaiccr lieutenant and— Ah! Here we go. Jita is the daughter of an underboss named Cuen. That was one of his residence compounds you raided to grab her."

"Cuen also has a presence on Kliseri-4," Doc read from his own terminal. "That's most likely who you were there to grab."

"It is likely his personal ship we stole," 701 said. "It was equipped for comfort, and an underboss would be accompanied by armed escort."

"Not to mention nobody in this sector would be stupid enough to attack him and bring the entire Vaiccr Syndicate down on their own heads," Mazer said.

"He's going to be pissed when he sees what you did to his ship," Twingo said.

"Yes, Twingo...people tend to get pissed off when they find out their personal vehicles were taken without their knowledge and crashed," Jason said, glaring at him. "One might even say it could push someone into a homicidal rage."

"We've got a good starting point here with this new information, but we need to work fast," Doc said. "If Ancula has this Cuen, he's close to executing his plan and ending Lucky's usefulness to him."

"Who is the lieutenant?" Jason asked.

"His name is Ligous," Doc said. "Why?"

"Let's talk to him." Jason shrugged. "He's gotta have some idea why Ancula is targeting his father. Let's try and make a deal with him."

"I like this idea. How do we find him?" Morakar asked.

"His dossier says he is currently on...Arospor-4. Same world as that compound you raided. Probably the same compound," Doc said.

"Shit," Jason hissed. "That could be a problem."

"Why?"

"A psychotic synth named Suta killed many of the Vissalo in the compound for sport," 701 said. "This Ligous may be among them."

"Still think it's our best shot," Jason said. "Let's get heading in that direction. Once Kage wakes up let him go through this all again, and we can adjust our plan from there as needed."

"This plan has a high probability of success," 701 said.

"Did...he just give the captain a compliment?" Twingo asked Doc.

"It would be wise to send the Galvetic warriors to make contact," 701 continued. "I will have certainly been seen, and they might have spotted someone of Captain Burke's stature despite the fact he was wearing armor, but nobody would mistake these three for anything other than what they are."

"Let's do it," Mazer said.

"How're things going with you? You look good."

"Thanks," Crusher said. "I feel great despite the fact I suspect Mazer is going to try and kill me at any moment."

"He's had plenty of time to do that if he was going to." Jason shrugged. "They must have some sort of plan to help you out of this mess."

"Maybe," Crusher said, leaning against the transit crate. They were standing in the cargo hold while Jason went through and inventoried what equipment had been on the ship when they'd fled S'Tora.

"Don't sound so eager to not get killed," Jason said.

"It's not that." Crusher waved him off. "I'm just still adjusting to being cut free. In all the years I've run with you on this crew, in the back of my mind, I was still the Guardian Archon of Galvetor. Now? I'll just be Crusher. I won't even be able to keep my own name."

"Seems like a lot to take in," Jason agreed. "Back before I climbed onto this ship when Deetz crashed in the mountains, I was just a separated staff sergeant. Nobody who would be missed or cared about. Certainly no sort of responsibility to my planet or country that would give me second thoughts. Answer me this; you knew how serious this was the same as I did, but you went through with it anyway. Why?"

"The idea of walking away from Omega Force hurt worse than the idea of walking away from Galvator, if you can believe that," Crusher said. "This is something I can live with."

"For what it's worth, I'm glad you picked us," Jason said, closing a crate and leaning against it. "I have no idea how long I can do this, but I sure as hell wouldn't want to do it without you guys."

"Where would you go if all of this ended?" Crusher asked.

"Not sure. Maybe Koliss-2 and see if Scout Fleet would want me as a technical advisor. Spend a little quality time with my kid when I get the chance. You?"

"You know, I have actually have no idea now. Before, I assumed I would just go back to Restaria and live out my last days fat and happy. With that option gone, S'Tora gone...who knows? Maybe go to Eshquaria."

"Not sure why we're even talking about retiring," Jason said. "With the ConFed gone, we're about to be a lot busier in the coming years. So many people fall through the cracks already, and that's about to get a whole lot worse."

"Can't wait."

27

"I see a dead man before me. How can that be?"

"How do you know I was dead, Cuen?" Ancula said.

"Because I saw your body," Cuen said. Lucky watched Ancula twitch at that but, otherwise, showed no emotion.

"You saw what I wanted you to see."

"Whatever. Why am I here, and why is Jita still a captive? You promised to release her if I came willingly."

"Still the soft spot for sweet little Jita," Ancula hissed. "Our kind's strength has always been not only the size of our family units but the understanding that sacrifice was acceptable as long as the family survived. She has always been your biggest weakness."

"I didn't realize I was so familiar to you, *Ancula*." Cuen sneered. "My interactions with you in the past were brief, almost in passing. You were a glorified accountant. Beneath my notice."

"Your bluster won't save you," Ancula said, turning to leave. "Lucky, please follow me out."

Lucky gave Cuen one last look before following Ancula out of the cell.

"I assumed he would be more forthcoming given how easily he was convinced to come with us," Lucky said.

"Oh, he will be," Ancula said. "This is all just posturing and keeping up appearances. He'll do anything to make sure Jita is unharmed. For now, we'll give him time to think about that."

Lucky wasn't so sure. He had a feeling that Cuen wasn't scared of Ancula and felt secure that he and his daughter were completely safe. The underboss's confidence in the fact Ancula was supposedly dead was also unnerving. Ancula gave a weak excuse as to why he was still around, but Lucky could tell Cuen didn't buy it. He needed to get in and talk to the prisoner alone somehow.

"What do you need from me?" he asked.

"As far as Cuen knows, you're still Seven, feared assassin and ruthless killer," Ancula said. "I want you to be the one who escorts him to and from his daughter's cell. I'm giving him two short visits a day. I need to let him see that she is my captive and subject to my whims. I want him to keep that firmly in mind when we begin to interrogate him."

"Schedule?"

"Your discretion. Just keep each visit under ten minutes."

"Understood."

Ancula walked away, muttering to himself. He looked rattled, and now Lucky wasn't certain what to make of the entire situation. If this Vissalo wasn't who he was claiming to be, then who was he? And who were the people he had abducted Lucky to help free? As he was running through the probabilities an orderly with a cart approached.

"Food for the prisoner," she said.

"I will take it in," Lucky said. "Thank you."

She looked relieved and left the brig as fast as she could. Lucky keyed the cell door open and took in just the tray of food, setting it on the table Cuen still sat behind. The Vissalo gangster watched him with that reptilian expression his species had that unnerved so many others.

"Seven, the most feared assassin in the quadrant...now serving meals to prisoners," Cuen said. "Fall on hard times?"

"If you wish to visit your daughter without a shattered jaw, it would be wise not to antagonize me," Lucky said, adopting Seven's speech mannerisms.

"When can I see her?"

"Eat, then I will take you. You will have ten minutes with her, nothing more."

Cuen ate quickly, keeping an eye on Lucky the entire time. Determining age was difficult with his species, but Cuen looked to be middle-aged and in good health. He was more muscular than most Vissalo and had a relaxed, confident air about him. Almost as if he knew something no one else did, and he was completely unconcerned with his current predicament.

"I'm ready."

"I will not bother with restraints," Lucky said. "If you do something foolish—"

"Your current boss wouldn't like it if you killed me." Cuen smirked.

"I have no need to kill you. You will be just as useful to my employer with or without functioning legs and arms."

"I see we understand each other. For what it's worth, I appreciate you not taking me to Jita in chains."

Lucky backed out of the cell and gestured for Cuen to follow. He Vissalo rose and walked out into the corridor, seeming to know exactly where he was going. Lucky found this curious but said nothing. A moment later, Cuen answered the question without being asked.

"Would you like to know how I know where Jita is being kept?" he asked. "Or how I know my way around this ship?"

"Not especially," Lucky said, knowing the underboss was going to talk regardless.

"One mistake your Ancula made was taking a ship that used to be in service with the syndicate," Cuen said. "I have been on this ship many times before."

"What was its purpose?" Lucky asked.

"Nothing nefarious. Light cargo with some modest tactical capability. Most of our operations are completely legal."

"I worked for Blazing Sun for a time. Their organization was much the same."

"Truly?" Cuen said in surprise. "Which of the Points did you work under?"

"I answered only to Saditava Mok himself," Lucky said.

"A shame what happened to his impressive organization," Cuen said. "He disappeared, likely assassinated, and it all fell into chaos. Once this is all over, perhaps you can come work for me."

"You are overly confident in your chances of surviving this."

"Hardly. Whoever this Vissalo is pretending to be Ancula—and it is a very convincing act—has made too many strategic blunders. I don't know what he is after, but the walls are closing in on him, and he likely doesn't realize it."

"Why tell me this?" Lucky asked.

"You seem like a smart...whatever you are. Strong survival instincts. If you ensure Jita's safety I will make certain you want for nothing for the rest of your life," Cuen said.

"We are here," Lucky said.

"You are coming in with me?"

"I must."

"Very well. But think about what I said, yes?"

"I heard you."

Lucky disengaged lock on the hatch and keyed it open to reveal a rather luxurious suite instead of a harsh brig cell. Cuen bobbed his head in approval and walked in.

"Jita?" he asked. "It is I...your father."

"Is this your doing?" an angry Vissalo female hissed as she came from the bedroom.

"Why would I have myself captured as well?" Cuen asked tiredly. "It is not my doing, but it is because of me. Our host thinks I know something, and he has abducted you to ensure I tell him."

"Is Ligous here as well?" Jita asked.

"No," Lucky answered, having no idea who that was. He wanted to try and get them to talk about something substantive during the short time they would be together.

"I thought your businesses were all completely legit these days," Jita accused.

"A mild exaggeration," Cuen said. "My sweet child, it is difficult to completely sanitize certain aspects of our operations. We have segregated as much as possible but, at the end of the day, we are who we are."

"And my brother and I live like prisoners in a compound because you fear something like this will happen."

"An unfortunate and temporary situation."

For the remaining eight minutes, they spoke of trivial, familial things, but Lucky detected a pattern in their speech. By the time it was over, he was certain they were speaking in code, but it was a cipher based on specific context rather than mathematics, so all he could do was listen, helpless to understand what they were really saying. By the time the conversation wrapped up, Jita seemed to have a steely resolve in her eyes that made Lucky nervous. What were they up to?

"Thank you for allowing me this time," Cuen said to him. "I am ready to return to my cell. I will require no further visits."

"An interesting conversation," Lucky said to him once they were out in the corridor again. He knew that the suite had full surveillance, but the corridors did not.

"Just some harmless reminiscing."

"Of course. I am certain that it was not a prearranged code and that you did not pass on instructions to your daughter that she acknowledged."

"You really must come work for me." Cuen laughed. "Such a remarkable being."

"I hope you have not set anything in motion that will put her life in danger."

"I would die before endangering her. Have you noticed how so many of the crew recognize who I am as we walk along?" Cuen asked abruptly. "They are bound to the ship. Ask your Ancula how the

M'aqu Family makes certain their non-Vissalo conscripts don't simply run off."

"Or you could just tell me now," Lucky said.

"Small explosive charges implanted near their spinal cords. If they leave the ship or their implant is manually triggered... You get the idea. This was a M'aqu ship that only occasionally flew routes for the syndicate. The Vaiccr Family's policy is that money is a better motivator than fear."

Lucky considered what he was just told and had to admit that it matched up with what he had observed on his own. Most of the crew on this ship were definitely not here of their own volition, nor did they harbor any particular loyalty to Ancula. He remained ensconced in the executive suite while Suta ensured nobody tried anything stupid.

"When you go to Ancula to report on our conversations, please tell him I request that he come down at his earliest convenience so we might get this over with as quickly as possible," Cuen said once they entered the brig.

"I will tell him," Lucky said. "Do you require anything between now and your evening meal?"

"Nothing at all, my unique friend," Cuen said, stretching out on the rack in his cell. "I'll just be here waiting."

———

"Pompous ass, isn't he?" Ancula asked once Lucky walked into the office.

"He is unusually confident for someone in his position," Lucky said.

"What did he talk to you about on your corridor walk?"

"He tried to offer me pay to ensure his daughter's safety," Lucky said.

"As expected," Ancula said. "He would wipe out entire planets for his precious Jita despite the fact she wouldn't lift a finger to save him were the roles reversed."

"Am I to assume that you have had previous dealings with this family?" Lucky asked.

"What does that matter to you?"

"My life is at risk in this mission. If you are emotionally compromised, then I need to know."

"You need to know what I tell you," Ancula said, now recomposed. He moved over and sat behind his desk, leaning back in the chair. "We depart for our target the moment Cuen gives up the information we need. I need you to go over to the other transport and make sure the merc teams are ready. My assumption is that this will be a ground assault with limited air support, but there's every possibility this will be a boarding action against an orbital platform."

"I will make certain they are as ready as can be," Lucky said, turning to leave.

"Suta will be going with you on the mission," Ancula said. "Make sure you have a place for him among the squads."

Lucky paused at the hatchway but said nothing. He walked out of the executive suite and encountered Suta a short way down the corridor. The synth moved to block his path.

"Get out of my way," Lucky said.

"You think I'm stupid?"

"Not *just* stupid. You are also insane."

"I see what you're doing. You think you can replace me? You can't. Ancula trusts me implicitly. He would never toss me aside for some uptight, preachy crusader like you," Suta said.

"Who are you trying to convince?" Lucky asked. "Me? Yourself?"

With that, he shoved Suta aside and continued down the corridor. He thought about stopping and speaking to Cuen one more time, but that seemed ill-advised. He needed to maintain the illusion that he was simply trying to do his job and leave.

As he passed crewmembers throughout the ship, he thought back to what Cuen had told him. All of them were here under duress, tied to the ship without the freedom to leave if they wished. The looks he observed ranged from haunted to resigned to angry, all of which now made sense in context.

"Can I assist you with anything, sir?"

Lucky looked and saw one of the medical staff that had helped him conceal the fact Kage had recovered.

"I am going to the hangar bay. I would not mind company."

"Of course, sir," the alien said, falling in beside him.

"Do you know a Vissalo named Cuen?" Lucky asked.

"He has traveled on this ship multiple times, though it has been some years. I have heard he is aboard as an unwilling guest at the moment."

"Is it true that most of the crew are also unwilling residents?"

"It is," the medic said without emotion. "We are pledged to the ship. It is simply the way things are. Do not waste your sympathy on us or any effort in a misguided attempt to free us. Just get yourself off this ship as quickly as you can and get as far away from the Vissalo as you can."

"It is not in my nature to abandon those who have helped me," Lucky said.

"Then, you will find yourself also a permanent resident. You have Ancula's favor at the moment, but that changes quickly."

"How did you become stuck here?"

"Many of us were purchased outright, others became indebted to the syndicate and thought they could work it off. Some even made deals to keep their family from harm. The thing we all have in common is that we thought we would only be here a short time. We were all wrong."

"Thank you for talking with me," Lucky said. "You should probably not be seen with me any further than this."

"Listen to what I have told you." He was practically pleading. "Run. Run and never look back."

The conversation left Lucky disgusted and confused. He agreed to help Ancula in order to secure the release of his friends. That had been accomplished.

So, why didn't he just kill the Vissalo and be done with it?

28

"I am looking for Ligous."

"Who are you?"

"Centurion Prime Mazer Reddix of the Galvetic Imperial Legion." This seemed to impress the Vissalo who had answered the gate. "Please, wait here, sir."

"Guardian Archon is more impressive than a Centurion Prime," Crusher muttered.

"And when they see a Galvetic warrior claiming to be someone who should be twenty years older than they look, what do you think would happen?" Morakar said.

"Centurion Reddix," a new Vissalo said, stepping through the gate. "I am Ligous. How might I help you? As you can imagine, it isn't every day we get a visit from the Galvetic Legions."

"This is unusual, I will admit," Mazer said. "We are part of a special intelligence detachment and have been tracking a Vissalo named Ancula over matters unrelated to your...family business."

"Ancula?"

"Of the M'aqu Family," Morakar provided.

"I'm aware of him. He'd disappeared for a while the last I heard. What has this to do with me?"

"He was responsible for the attack on your home," Mazer said. "He has also abducted Cuen, who we believe is your father."

"Please, come in," Ligous said, nodding to his people.

The warriors went through a quick security scan before moving into the walled compound. Mazer walked up to the Vaiccr lieutenant and crashed his fist to his chest before extending the hand. Ligous looked confused but grasped the hand with his own. Mazer reached with his left hand and grabbed the Vissalo's forearm, shaking the arm vigorously. The guards perked up at that, but their boss waved them off.

"What interest does the Galvetic Empire have with a single Vissalo?" Ligous asked, pulling forcefully to extricate his arm.

"That's classified, unfortunately," Mazer said. "But it has to do with some irregular accounting issues on a planet we have a protection treaty with."

"That sounds right," Ligous said. "The attack on my home had been a mystery as was the abduction of my sister. If my father is also missing, I suspect she was taken for leverage. Unfortunately, Ancula unleashed a force that killed many of my men, most needlessly so."

"In the course of our investigation, we've learned that Ancula has become wholly obsessed with freeing a group he calls his family," Mazer said. "We think he has taken Cuen because he does not actually know where they are being held."

"Interesting. Ancula has no family. None who are alive, at least. Is it possible you are mistaken?"

"It's possible he doesn't mean an actual familial relation," Crusher said.

"Possible, but hardly something I would know," Ligous said. "I'm sorry to say you may have made the trip for nothing. I have no information that will be of use to you. If you'll excuse me, I have much to do here in the wake of the attack on my home."

"You don't seem very concerned about your father and sister being abducted," Crusher remarked.

"You would need to understand Vissalo familial dynamics, my Galvetic friend. Good luck on your mission."

Ligous walked off, and his security stepped in front of the Galvetics in what was an obvious invitation for them to leave. They turned and allowed themselves to be escorted off the property. Crusher took note of the newly installed gate and fresh repairs on the stonework of the walls after Jason's mortar attack.

"Success?" he asked after they were out of earshot of the gate sentries.

"We shall see," Mazer said.

"...the hell is the Galvetic Empire doing sniffing around this?"

"I don't know, sir. I do know they're who they say they were. Feature recognition confirms that two of them were Mazer Reddix and Morakar Reddix, both high-ranking members in the Galvetic Legions, but not known to be attached to their intelligence service."

"The intelligence operative was probably the third, younger one you didn't get a hit on."

"Audio clarity is outstanding," Kage remarked. "They must be in an unshielded room."

While Mazer had genuinely been trying to pull any information he could out of Ligous during their meeting, his real goal had been to make as much direct contact as possible so Kage's batch of nanobot listening devices could transfer onto the Vissalo. Hundreds of the tiny machines had latched onto his clothing and were now broadcasting to a relay station one of Kage's micro-drones had flown up to the top of the compound wall.

"Do we have any idea where my sister and father are?" Ligous asked.

"No," an underling said.

"I don't have any choice. We need to warn Maribel that Cuen may be compromised and that Ancula could be heading their way," Ligous said.

"Maribel?" the underling asked.

"Ancula is looking to free someone we're holding as leverage. If he took my father, it means he has narrowed it down to one of the facilities we control. What I know that Ancula does not is that Maribel is the only one of the five we control who is currently active," Ligous said. "If he has my sister as well, Cuen will not risk playing games and giving him false information."

"I will inform them of a pending attack immediately," the underling said. The audio became garbled, and then the signal from all the bugs cut out at the same time.

"He must have gone into a shielded room," Kage said.

"Will we get the signal back if he comes back out?" Jason asked.

"Nope. They're programmed to shut down when they lose contact with the relay station and, before you ask, I'm already running Maribel through our sources."

Hours of exhaustive searching through their usual sources turned up nothing on the name. They cross-referenced Cuen with known private prisons within the Vaiccr territory, but still nothing. Kage was becoming visibly angry, not used to being stonewalled. Normally, he was able to pick up the scent with much less than a name and begin digging up actionable intel but, for this, he had nothing.

"Has to be a codename," Doc said.

"If it is, it's a well-kept secret," Kage said.

They continued to work, but Jason could tell that the team was losing energy and focus. Just as he was about to recommend they break for the night and come back at it fresh, something caught his eye as the data scrolled across his screens. It was in a list of assets that the Vaiccr Family controlled, and he almost missed it.

Mar I'bel.

. . .

Could they really be chasing their tails because of a translation error? It was such a rare thing to encounter that nobody ever thinks to check for it. With renewed excitement, he punched in the new search parameters, and the Zadra Network began spitting out results almost immediately. Mar I'bel was an ancient fortress on the planet Kulack Major. It had been used by the Vaiccr Family for over a hundred years for various purposes. One of the reports from the network showed that it was currently controlled by a Vissalo named Cuen.

"Holy shit," he said. "I found it."

"You?" Kage snorted. "Doubtful."

"Read it and weep you little shit," Jason said, moving the search results onto the main canopy for everyone to look at.

"Damnit," Kage whispered as they all looked over the information and saw the images of the imposing stone structure.

"Now, we need to find our who or what is in it that Ancula would want," Doc said.

"We can do that en route," Jason said. "Let's get her airborne and heading for the Kulack System."

Jason and Kage brought the flight systems online while the others filtered off the bridge to continue working or rest. Since the *Phoenix* had been sitting on the ramp in standby and not completely shut down, it only took minutes to fire the engines and get her into the air. The ride up to orbit was quick and mercifully uneventful.

"You have it from here?" Kage asked. "I'm going back to the com room to start pulling everything I can on Mar I'bel."

"Go for it," Jason said. "We'll be meshing-out in a couple of hours and then I'm crashing for a while. It looks like we have a four day flight to Kulack so we won't have a ton of time to prep."

"It'll be enough," Kage hopped out of his seat. "We'll be ready. Probably."

"Comforting," Jason said.

Alone on the bridge and with nothing pressing to do, the events from the last few weeks pressed in on him. His immediate concern was getting Lucky back and eliminating Ancula as a threat, probably killing Suta as well for good measure. But he also had to consider what the future held for him and the crew. Losing S'Tora was a devastating blow. It was a world they'd put down deep roots in. A place they loved and talked about retiring permanently to. Getting tossed back into the life of nomadic hired guns might not be something all of them would be excited about.

"At least I've still got you," he said to the *Phoenix* as the sound of the engines lulled him to sleep.

29

"Kulack Major. Beautiful world, is it not?"

"I suppose," Lucky said. "Does not seem to be the sort of world our target would be on."

"To be honest, I'm surprised as well," Ancula said. "Mar I'bel has been in the hands of the Vaiccr Family for a long time, but it was never really used for anything. It was a dramatic venue for their parties and meetings but little more. When Cuen took over this territory, he must have seen more potential for the old fortress."

"A prison right under everyone's nose," Lucky said. "Clever."

"Indeed. All the security would seem natural given the nature of the meetings here. Half the detainees probably came here on a guest list at one time, never to leave."

The ship was sitting in high orbit, flying an entirely different registry, and her profile had been altered using what smugglers call *decoy flaps*. Large sections of alloy could be deployed and configured to fool the automatic identification protocols for most orbital control systems. They wouldn't pass a close visual inspection, but it would amount of Lucky trying to smooth it over helped. After talking with Ancula about it, he had shifted his opinion that the Vissalo was inexperienced with this sort of operation and put far too much trust in Suta that he knew what to do. He hired more mercs than he needed, and then let the synth amuse himself by screwing with them while he waited for his timetables to align.

"Is that crazy-ass thing coming with us?" the merc asked, pointing to Suta as the synth walked off the shuttle.

"Unfortunately," Lucky said. "He should not be a problem, but tell your people to watch their backs around him."

"Will do."

"Why is everyone just standing around?" Suta demanded.

"The ship has not even begun to deorbit," Lucky said. "What would you have them doing?"

"Just have them ready when we land," Suta said, walking off.

"You watch your back, too," the merc standing with Lucky said. "I don't think he's coming down to help on the mission."

"Hey! Wake up!"

"Fuck off," Jason said and rolled back over.

"T'Cali Amon is on the com. He sent the request himself."

"Cool. Tell him to fuck off, too," Jason grumbled sleepily.

Crusher, apparently done with being nice, grabbed Jason by his clothes and snatched him off his rack and tossed him through the hatch, where he sprawled onto the deck with a pained grunt.

"Are you awake now?" he asked calmly.

"I'm going to allow that because I know you're going through a lot," Jason groaned, climbing to his feet.

He padded through the main deck in his bare feet and up the stairs to the command deck where he found Doc chatting with Amon in the com room via a hyperlink connection. The hardware had been gifted to them by Earth and was lightyears ahead of the ubiquitous slip-com. Once Earth released it for general use, it would revolutionize communication and data networking throughout the quadrant, not to mention make his homeworld a shit ton of money.

"Did I wake you?" Amon asked when he saw Jason's disheveled state.

"Technically, Crusher did, and he wasn't gentle about it," Jason said. "What's up?"

"Similan brought to my attention your recent reports regarding the Vissalo named Ancula you're tracking," Amon said. "We definitely know he's not the real Ancula. That person was killed by our operatives in a botched raid on a Vissalo data center some years back."

"Botched?" Jason asked.

"The center was supposed to be empty of people. Our forces hit the location and found that the real Ancula had been using it as a secret meeting location. All the equipment helped mask them from sensors and made remote surveillance virtually impossible. Everyone there was killed. Our people removed all evidence they were ever there so, as far as the Vaiccr Syndicate was concerned, they just disappeared. Imagine our surprise when another Ancula popped up right after you shut down the operation at The Gates."

"I have to say I'm a little surprised at how open you're being about this," Jason said.

"I need to be perfectly clear because of how important what I'm about to tell you is," Amon said. "After seeing that the target was Mar I'bel, we now feel confident that whoever this Ancula really is, he plans on trying to release a quintet of Vissalo bosses called the Dagari, which roughly translates to *Old Fathers* or *Founders*, depending on which dialect you're using."

"And these Dagari are bad?" Jason asked.

"They have the power and influence to fully unite the Vissalo syndicates. It would be like having an organization as far-reaching as Blazing Sun at its peak but ruled by people like Bondrass and with no ConFed to keep them in check," Amon said. "They would quickly become the dominant criminal power in the quadrant that would

30

"Mar I'bel has defenses that are biased toward an orbital or aerial attack. They will not expect this."

"So, you say," the transport captain said as the heavily armored troop carriers rolled out of his hold. "I'll remain here per the contract, but I don't expect I'll be taking too many survivors back to Enzola-2."

Lucky said nothing as the six armored vehicles lined up and the mercs began climbing aboard. The vehicles were far too conspicuous to take down public roadways to Mar I'bel, which was nearly seventy kilometers away, so they would be loaded up onto commercial freight haulers and disguised.

"I will not be returning to the ship, so do not wait for me," Lucky said. "Once the time limit is up after the first vehicle arrives, depart at once."

"You don't have to tell me twice," the captain said. "Good luck with whatever the hell you're doing."

The freight haulers arrived only a few minutes late and were let onto the private landing pad after a quick security check. The armored vehicles were loaded onto the low-slung cargo sleds and quickly covered in such a way that broke up their shape. Lucky did one final check before moving toward the first vehicle where he would ride.

"I will go in this one," Suta said, pointing to the fifth in line. That vehicle was the one with the heavy cannon turret mounted on top and was critical to breaching the perimeter. Lucky hesitated, not sure why he picked that one, but he didn't want to give Suta the impression he cared where he was at all.

"Why are you telling me?" he asked. "I do not care where you go, just so long as you stay out of the way."

"I wouldn't worry about that," Suta said. "I have my own mission."

Lucky pondered that as he boarded his own vehicle and signaled to the haulers that they were ready to depart. What mission could Suta possibly have if he was sent down specifically for Lucky to kill? Or was this just more of Suta's usual games? The synth was unstable and, in addition to his love of indiscriminate killing, he also was fond of psychological torment.

"We are ready," Lucky said to the driver of the first troop carrier, who nodded and signaled to all the haulers. The large, automated vehicles pulled away from the transport, heading for the main gate. The trip to Mar I'bel would be less than an hour, and then the assault would be over in half that. If they couldn't breach in thirty minutes and get to the detention area, they couldn't do it at all. They simply didn't have enough troops or vehicles for a prolonged fight.

It was almost over.

The haulers moved them along on the dedicated commercial roadway, which was far less crowded than the civilian roads, getting them to the interchange in forty-five minutes. Mar I'bel was just visible in the distance as the vehicles rolled ponderously off the commercial route and up onto an older, bumpier civil road that was probably a few centuries old. The road would take them right by the ancient fortress and was traversed often enough their convoy shouldn't attract too much attention until it was too late.

"Ten seconds!" the driver called. "Starting engines."

A few seconds after the engines thrummed to life, the driver steered to the right and slammed the accelerators down. The big, armored carrier leapt off the moving vehicle, tearing through its concealment, and slamming into the roadway. The entrance to the compound was a mere two hundred meters ahead, so the driver had to lean on the brakes while maintaining control, steering into the wide entrance lane and right toward the closed gates and stunned guards.

"Gunners!" Lucky barked. "Open fire!"

Autocannons on articulated mounts opened up, shredding the guards and blasting the gatehouse to rubble. The driver accelerated and blasted through the gate, setting off the anti-personnel mines that had been embedded in its decorative surface. The mines hadn't been designed to handle a full-blown armored war machine, so the carrier suffered minimal damage.

"All vehicles check in," Lucky said over the com.

"Two."

"Four"

"Six."

"Five."

"Vehicle three, check in," Lucky said.

"Three checking in."

"Form up and begin primary assault."

There was still one, much more substantial gate to breach before they made it onto the main property itself. The vehicles formed up into two columns and raced toward it at full speed, peppering it with cannon fire to keep the guards off balance. There were two vehicles mounted with large plasma cannons on turrets, essentially a scaled down version of a starship cannon. They couldn't fire rapidly, but they caused heavy damage. The pair of specialized vehicles were in the second row, shielded and hidden by the front. Once they were within range, the front two vehicles pulled to either side, and the big cannons belched out brilliant blue-white streaks of superheated plasma. The inner gate and most of the right support column was vaporized, as were all the defending troops.

"Anti-mine countermeasures," Lucky ordered.

From the top of the two lead vehicles, hundreds of tiny, dart-like munitions were launched, cascading down on the area around the gates. Each little dart packed a small explosive warhead that would go off on contact, designed to trip or destroy any mines buried beneath the roadbed.

"Two secondary explosions," the gunner reported. "Road is still navigable."

"Proceed to primary objective, still condition alpha," Lucky said.

The vehicles barreled through the smoking wreckage of the gate as the first alarms wailed across the property. Mar I'bel was an imposing monolith as they sped toward it. Fifty meters past the gate, the vehicles redeployed with two veering off to take out the aerial defense systems with the other four moving to neutralize ground security.

"Number Five, get back in formation," Lucky heard his driver say. His head snapped over to the tactical display in front of the gunner in time to see the fifth vehicle—the one Suta had climbed aboard—veer from the main formation. He had a sinking feeling at what was about to happen.

"We're being targeted!" the gunner said just as the plasma cannon fired.

The impact was horrendous. Armor was boiled away, and the vehicle was flipped off its wheels. It slammed back into the turf and slid down an embankment, disappearing off the edge into the lake that took up the southeast corner of the compound.

Lucky looked around and saw that most of the mercs had survived but were still injured from being bounced around in their harnesses. The driver was clearly dead, and the gunner had been impaled by one of the control sticks thanks to his harness being too loose.

"Who is still alive?" he asked. There was a chorus of groans and waved hands. "Get out of your harnesses if you can. This vehicle is sinking, and we must exit immediately."

The less injured helped the severely injured out of their harnesses. The dead were left as they were. The vehicle pitched over twenty degrees to the left, and water was just beginning to seep in through the outer seals. He looked at the battered mercs and realized most probably wouldn't be able to make it up to the surface depending on how deep the water was, but they certainly couldn't stay inside either.

"I am going to open the pressure equalization valves first to let the water in. It will happen quickly. Once the water is nearly to the roof, I will jettison the dorsal hatches, fore and aft. They will be ringed by a bright, white light. Swim toward it and push yourselves to the surface. Help each other to the banks, and then stay there."

"Are you going to go kill the fucker that shot us?" someone from the back asked.

"Yes," Lucky said. "Now, standby."

He pulled the lever to blow the valves, and pyrotechnic charges fired to jam them permanently open. Water came flooding in quickly from multiple points, and he watched the mercs as it rose past their chests.

"Eyes closed, mouths open!" he called. "As soon as the hatches blow, close your mouths and swim to the surface!"

Before any of them could say anything, he blew the hatches. In water, they didn't lift very far before the rocket motors kicked, blasting the interior of the cabin with exhaust before they slowly spiraled away and letting the water rush in. He began grabbing disoriented mercs and pushing them up through the openings. It took him less than fifteen seconds to push them all up through the opening and make sure they were kicking for the surface. He took one last look at the dead before pushing himself through a hatchway and firing his repulsors. He rocketed up to the surface, blasting up and out of the lake. He stopped at a low hover to make sure the survivors were taking care of each other before locating the second vehicle in his formation.

Suta had apparently only been targeting Lucky's vehicle because the second one was already at the objective, engaged with local troops for control of Mar I'bel's aerial defense system. He shot off toward them, switching to combat mode and deploying his cannons. Coming in from above the fray, he could clearly see how the enemy was dug in and opened fire, his plasma cannons ripping into the stunned troops. They screamed and fell back, allowing the mercs to press forward.

Rallying after the arrival of Lucky, they were able to secure the main entrance. Lucky landed and walked up to the squad leader.

"Resistance?"

"Minimal, but well-trained. Any survivors for you?"

"Yes, but not combat effective," Lucky said. "Let's clear this room and begin setting charges. We're falling behind."

The squad tossed grenades through the doorway, one after another, and twenty in all. The staggered concussive blasts actually started to weaken the structure as the walls shook and bulged with each hit. The screams had stopped after the first three, but Lucky had them use the whole case before the squad moved in to clear out survivors. He moved in with them, moving quickly to the system's weak point. The controls for the aerial defense were inside the fortress, but the power to feed the sensors and guns routed through a junction that they were about to blow.

It wasn't the main power feed to the fortress, and the designers likely didn't recognize the vulnerability when they were adding it to the ancient structure, assuming that if an attack made it this far, then they'd lost the battle already. The junction supplied power to all the perimeter gun emplacements that were currently still retracted and hidden as well as the main targeting array that was cleverly disguised as an arboretum at the north end of the main compound. Once it was taken out, the operators inside would try to reroute power but would be unable to do so. Ancula would be clear to land once they pulled the five Vissalo he wanted from confinement without fear of being shot down.

"Charges set. Get clear!"

Everyone ran from the building as the timed charges fired, cleanly severing the heavy power cables and probably blowing out the overload protection in the main building. There would be no quick fix to get the aerial defense up, and the Vaiccr were about to learn a lesson about hardening all power and control lines.

"Load up!" Lucky shouted.

They had taken no casualties and only a few injuries taking out the power junction. The armored troop carrier roared away toward where the other four should have already breached the main building. When they got around the edge, however, it appeared things had gone badly.

"What the..." The driver was looking at bodies everywhere, merc and Vissalo, along with three burned out hulks that used to be armored troop carriers leaving just one intact.

"Looks like they've breached," the gunner said. "Hell of a fight."

"Perhaps," Lucky said, noticing that the undamaged vehicle was the one Suta had used to blast them into the lake. "Pull up behind the remaining vehicle. We must proceed carefully, but quickly."

When the rear ramp dropped, the sounds of heavy fighting from inside reached their ears. Lucky motioned them forward as the group readied their weapons and advanced. There was a hole blasted into the side of the building that showed, underneath the stonework, there was a substantial layer of alloy armor. It was a good thing he opted for heavy cannons to breach rather than explosives. The cannon could fire as long as it had power, whereas explosives were one and done.

The blast marks on the walls and the angle of the hits on the ground indicated they were engaged by emplacements along the top of the wall and took them out with the autocannons on the other vehicles. There were also a lot of dead Vissalo strewn about with the bodies of the mercs, meaning they'd sent a force to directly engage.

Apparently, Suta was among the survivors since he didn't see the wretched synth's body anywhere.

"Be aware that the other synth, the one named Suta, should be engaged on sight," Lucky said. "He is the one who opened fire on the lead vehicle and killed our comrades. You are clear to take him out... if I do not get to him first."

They moved in through the breach in the wall with no idea what they'd find inside.

31

"There's Ancula's ship."

"Which one?" Jason asked.

"Highlighting it now," Kage said. "Different codes and some half-assed smuggler's sails deployed, but that's definitely it. *Phoenix* got a good look at her back at The Gates."

"There's a flight of combat shuttles leaving the ship and heading for the surface," Doc said. "Think Lucky is on one of them?"

"Our first pass showed that Mar I'bel is already under attack," Kage said. "I'd bet this is the recovery team going down to pick up the Dagari."

"Let's not spook them just yet," Jason said. "I know we all want to get down there, but let's not make a bad situation worse by bumbling in blind and without knowing where Lucky is."

"Wise," 701 approved. Crusher and Kage just looked at him, and then each other.

"I liked it better when you two took shots at each other," Crusher said. "This newfound respect and cooperation is boring."

"Can you plot me an entry vector that trails those shuttles, but doesn't look like it's trailing the shuttles?" Jason asked.

"Already working on it," Kage said. "I can track them through the orbital control system, and then we can drop down well south of them and fly to Mar I'bel directly. It'll be a little slower within the atmosphere, but they won't even notice us."

"Sending helm control to you," Jason said. "Your show."

The *Phoenix* smoothly changed course, jumping through the transfer orbits in a way that wouldn't look unusual. The formation of combat shuttles actually passed above them on their way to a direct entry vector while the Jepsen gunship flew a conventional approach for the southern hemisphere. Jason took the opportunity to scan the three with what would appear to them to be nothing more than a navigational array and what he saw made him frown. All three were newer Aracorian Type-15 combat shuttles, which were top of the line. He could only assume they were fully loaded, which meant plasma cannons, missiles, and an impressive defensive system suite.

"Wish we had a little more firepower with us," he said, looking at his armament panel. All of the energy weapons were freshened up and fully charged, but their expendable munitions were woefully inadequate. When Twingo had torn her down, he had taken everything but the XTX-4 ship busters and two racks of their Pixie missiles out of the weapons bays. He hadn't been able to replace them before S'Toran authorities chased them off the planet.

"Entering the atmosphere in twenty," Kage said. "Ground team might want to put on their party hats."

"If I got dragged all this way and don't get to shoot someone in the face, I'm going to be very angry," Crusher said as he stomped off the bridge.

The fighting inside the walls of Mar I'bel was intense, and Lucky realized right away he hadn't enough troops to come out on top. To their credit, the guild mercs were fighting with everything they had with little regard for their lives. But it wasn't enough.

They had descended into the lower level, deciding to push for the detention level fast before the Vaiccr realized what they were there for. The plan had worked well enough, but the numbers just weren't on their side, and they were being pushed back into a corner. There was no sign of Suta, and Lucky was completely blocked off by weapons fire from an unknown source to get to the cellblock the objectives were housed in. He was about to call for a strategic withdrawal to rally and organize his forces when something strange happened.

The walls shook, and dust rained down as something hammered away on the structure above. The bombardment intensified, and the floors shook so hard many of the mercs couldn't keep their footing and hit the ground. This went on for the next few minutes, and then everything went silent. No enemy fire from ahead and nothing hitting the building from above.

"That will do, everyone. Please, come outside so we can get this sorted," a voice came over the building's intercom.

"Who the hell was that?" one of the mercs asked.

"That would be our employer," Lucky said. "We've been set up."

"What do we do?"

"We comply. For now," Lucky told them. "Drop your weapons at the entry point, and then walk out and do not make any threatening moves. Do nothing that will prompt him to kill you sooner than he plans."

"Damn, this job sucks," someone complained as they trudged back down the corridor.

When Lucky walked out into the light, he could see a combat shuttle sitting on the ground, with two more hovering above and behind. Ancula stood there with no expression, along with twenty armored troopers from his ship. There was a shimmer in the air that indicated he was behind active shielding.

"What is this?" Lucky called across the spanning distance, motioning for his mercs to settle down behind him. There was movement along the north wall, and he turned to see Suta and four of Ancula's troopers escorting five Vissalo who were old enough that their skin looked dull and rough instead of the usually glistening, vibrant green.

"I wish you had decided to join me, Lucky. I really do," Ancula said sadly. "Think of what we could have accomplished together. For what it's worth, I didn't want it to turn out like this. I wanted you as a partner, but now you're only useful as a scapegoat."

"Who are you really?" Lucky asked.

"This isn't a conversation, my friend," Ancula said. "Once they're on board, we'll be—" One of the hovering shuttles exploded in a brilliant fireball, sending out a shockwave that knocked everyone except Lucky and Suta to the ground. The second shuttle turned, but it exploded as well. Lucky turned in time to see the *Phoenix* coming up from the south. The gunship roared over Mar I'bel, pulling into a hard climb just as the hulk of the second shuttle spun and hit close to the one that had been on the ground, damaging its starboard side.

The ground was still shaking from the *Phoenix*'s engines as all hell broke loose. Ancula's troopers circled around him and ran for the armored vehicle Lucky had left parked away from the wall breach. Suta turned and ran back toward the fortress, the five Vissalo hot on his heels. He let them go and focused his fire on the armored vehicle, taking out the targeting sensors and the autocannon mounts so they couldn't be used against the surviving mercs. The vehicle never opened fire, only turned around and raced back down the main drive. Lucky was about to fire his repulsors and pursue when the *Phoenix* reappeared, coming around the building in a low hover with her nose pitched slightly up.

"Lucky!" Jason's voice boomed from the external speakers. "Let him go! We need those five old lizards your buddy took. They cannot be allowed to escape!"

Lucky had no idea how Jason knew who they were, but he trusted his captain completely. He turned and ran after Suta.

"Arm yourselves!" he shouted to the mercs. "Get ready to retreat in the vehicle."

With that, he fired his repulsors and took off, arcing around the building and trying to track where Suta had gone, determined to finish the job and kill the insane synth.

"Put us down right there," Jason said before running off the bridge.

"Then, what?" Kage shouted after him.

"Try to find Ancula!"

The *Phoenix* settled into a low hover so Jason, Crusher, Mazer, Morakar, and 701 could ride the transit beam down. As soon as the battlesynth's feet hit the ground, the gunship wheeled around and climbed away, searching for the armored vehicle that had just fled the area.

"You and I should pursue Lucky, the Galvetic warriors can wrangle the mercs into a defensible position," 701 said, already moving away. Jason looked at Crusher and shrugged before taking off after him.

It had been easy to spot where they had re-entered the fortress structure at. There was a doorway on the northside that had been blown out from the inside. 701 switched to full combat mode and went in first, Jason switched his ocular implants to low-light mode and followed. He wasn't wearing armor, so he didn't have the benefit of sensors, but he did have his trusty railgun in his hand, so he still felt good about the whole thing.

"You have the trail, Lassie?" he asked.

"You are not amusing," 701 said, swinging his head around like a dog looking for the scent. In reality, he was scanning the area with the mid-range sensors that were in his cranium. "They went this way."

"Lead on."

They raced down the wide corridor that looked like it had been built much more recently than the stone castle above them. It curved to the left with many side passages, but 701 kept on charging past them, clearly picking up something ahead.

"You sure this is the right way?" Jason asked. A moment later, they heard the exchange of weapons fire and an explosion, followed by Lucky flying out of a side passage and slamming into the wall, trailing smoke.

"Reasonably certain," 701 said.

"Stay back!" Lucky said when he saw them, climbing to his feet and diving away as more plasma shots hit the wall where he'd just been.

"So...how's it going?" Jason asked as his friend joined them.

"I have been better," Lucky said, his armor discolored and still smoking. "He upgraded his weaponry to include a small missile launcher, but I believe that is his last shot."

"Any idea where that passage leads?" Jason asked.

"I believe there is a subterranean garage with various vehicles inside," Lucky said.

"Shit. We can't let him get away. I'll explain later, but we have to capture or kill those five Vissalo no matter what."

"Understood. Let us proceed. Captain, please remain behind us as you are not wearing armor."

"No argument there," Jason said.

701 and Lucky approached the passageway and opened fire. They executed a move called "rounding the corner," where 701 used the cover of the walls to provide suppressing fire while allowing Lucky to move against the back wall and get an angle farther down while minimizing exposure behind the covering fire. Suta had apparently been waiting for them to try something like that and responded with overwhelming fire into both the far wall and the corner 701 was using for cover. The amount of plasma fire, smoke, and dust overwhelmed Jason's eyes, so he switched to long-wave infrared to cut through the airborne particles.

He kneeled down and spotted one of the Dagari huddled against the wall. Taking aim, he squeezed off a round, hitting the Vissalo center-mass. The hypersonic round left a vortex in its wake and blew the target into three pieces. Amazingly, a second of the Dagari, still blind in the dark passage, came over to see what happened. As he probed blindly around in the goop that had been his friend, Jason shot him as well, turning him into a similar mess of bone and blood.

"I got two of them," Jason shouted. "You see the other three?"

"They are behind a cluster of alloy conduits," Lucky said, moving away from the opening.

"You bastards!" Suta shouted. "You stupid bastards!"

"He sounds pissed." Jason laughed.

"Here he comes," 701 said, backing away as Suta charged them, firing his cannons as fast as he could. Before he made it to the main corridor, however, his power system suffered a catastrophic failure, likely from overheating, and he stumbled out into the open, trying to pull the smoking, sparking cannons from his arms.

"I have waited a long time for this," Lucky said.

"As have I," 701 agreed. Suta looked up and seemed surprised, just realizing that he'd rushed headlong into their midst with no functioning weapons.

"You self-righteous fools," he hissed. "Do you know what you have done? Do you know what Ancula will do to you when he finds out?"

"Right now, I'd be more worried about what these two are going to do to you," Jason said.

Lucky and 701 approached slowly, splitting apart and covering any avenue of escape the damaged synth might take.

"You think I'm afraid of you?" Suta asked, laughing insanely.

"Of course, you are," Lucky said, leaping forward and slamming a fist into Suta's face, smashing the cranial plating and damaging the right eye to the point it hung uselessly. Suta screamed and tried to turn and flee only to be met by 701's fist, smashing the other side of his head. The armor plating held this time, but it still must have caused significant damage. The synth's screams sounded garbled as he seemed to lose control of his legs and fell to the ground.

Lucky and 701 looked at each other, the latter motioning for the other to proceed and stepping back. The battlesynth that used to be called Combat Unit 777, someone who had gone through hell multiple times in his life including dying and being reborn as someone else, would finally be able to put one of his demons to rest.

"For the people of Pyriat-2," he said solemnly. He slammed a foot down on Suta's right thigh to hold him down and grabbed the head, pulling up as hard as he could. Lucky's actuators strained and whined as they went to full power until, with a tortured shriek of rending metal, Suta's head came off in a shower of sparks.

"Now, it is over," 701 said.

"Not quite," Jason said, gesturing to the three old Vissalo groping their way down the passage trying to escape. "Shall we?"

"You cannot hit them from here with that ridiculous weapon?" 701 asked.

"Sure. But shouldn't we keep one or two alive? Eshquarian Intelligence would probably pay handsomely for them."

"They are a threat if left alive," 701 said. "Are you willing to put the safety of your crewmates in the hands of the Empire?"

"Good point," Jason said, hefting his weapon and taking aim... then lowered it again. "Doesn't seem very sporting."

"You wish to bludgeon them to death with your fists instead?" 701 asked. "You are the one who insisted they need to die. Is there any morality in *how* they die? Kill them."

"Damnit," Jason sighed. "Let's go get one of them. There are going to be reprisals for all this. We need to know what might be coming our way."

"Another wise decision," 701 said, looking at Lucky and nodding.

32

"It's like they just disappeared," Doc said.

"This guy probably had more than one contingency plan," Kage said. "Swing around and make one more pass down the eastern roadway. They obviously ditched the armored carrier, but where?"

"Does it matter?" Twingo asked.

"It does if we want to find this guy," Kage said.

"He has to go back to his ship. We know where that is." Twingo shrugged. "The main cannons would make short work of a ship not expecting an attack."

"No!" Kage said sharply. "We are not attacking that ship."

"Why not?" Doc asked. "We've done worse for less justification."

"The crew of that ship is innocent," Kage insisted. "It'd be little different than strafing that town down there."

"Whatever," Twingo said. "Then, you think of something since you're apparently calling the shots here."

"We need to head toward that ship," Kage said.

"Oh, for fuck's sake," Twingo said, using one of Jason's favorite expressions. "Make up your mind!"

"Not to shoot it down," Kage said, feeding course data to Doc in the pilot seat. "I developed something while I was aboard but wasn't in a position to deploy it. With Ancula and Suta off the ship, I might be able to convince them to upload it and free themselves."

"What are you even— You know what? Doesn't matter," Doc said. "Heading up."

He pulled the *Phoenix* into a vertical climb and shoved the power up, sending her rocketing toward space. The new holographic display Twingo had installed displayed data in three dimensions near the canopy so he could see the sensor data overlaid with the view outside.

"Why do we need to get close?" Doc asked.

"I need to use a proximity channel," Kage said. "I don't have any private com access to that ship and don't want to broadcast on local coms. If Ancula catches wind what I'm up to, he may trigger the charges."

"What charges?" Twingo asked.

"Every crewmember up there has an explosive charge in them. They're slaves to the ship. If they leave or simply displease Ancula in any way...pop."

"Vissalo," Doc said, making the word sound like a curse. "Their criminal cartels are the most ruthless in the galaxy, but this is a whole new level."

"Just get me within fifty klicks, and I'll handle the rest," Kage said.

———

"How many more can they have left?"

"No idea," Mazer said. "I've never been here."

"That was rhetorical, moron," Crusher said. "And what the hell are you doing down there? Is that soup?"

"It's blood. *Your* blood," Mazer said, pulling two medical bags out of his pack with the dark purple blood in it.

"What the hell are you doing with my blood?!"

"He's going to throw it on the enemy and hope they catch a few of

"Then, what?" the officer asked.

"Then, you do what you want. Take the ship and leave," Doc said. "Get to safe harbor, leave it there and go your own way. No matter what you do, get the hell out of Vissalo territory as fast as you can."

"Activate the package," the first officer said to the medic.

When Kage had first made contact, it took a moment to get past the captain, who had to be detained by his own crew. Apparently, he was a loyalist despite the fact he was a veritable slave with a bomb in his head. Maybe he didn't think of himself as such, or maybe he actually wasn't tied to the ship. Either way, the bridge crew took care of him.

"I think it worked," the first officer said. "The chief engineer reports the control unit has shut down, but there's no way to verify that. It's locked in a tamper-proof cage."

"This is the best I can do for you," Kage said. "Unfortunately, I have no way to verify with absolute certainty whether it worked or not."

"I will talk it over with the senior staff and determine how we want to proceed. I thank you for your efforts regardless of what happens."

"You'll need to decide quickly. We lost track of Ancula on the surface, and he's certainly going to be heading your way as soon as he makes it to a ship," Twingo said. "Good luck."

"Let's get back down there," Doc said, pulling the *Phoenix* away from ship. "We grab our friends, and we get as far away from here as we can."

33

"Sir, we are prepped for departure, but we have lost contact with the ship."

"What do you mean you lost contact?" Ancula snarled. "Why aren't they answering?"

"They're not answering because they're not there," the shuttle pilot said, cowering away from his clearly enraged boss. "When we couldn't raise them on coms, we checked the navigation beacon. They no longer appear in the system."

"How is that even possible?"

"If the ship left and locked us out of the remote links, or..."

"Or what?" Ancula snapped.

"Or it was destroyed."

Ancula paused at that. Would Lucky's crew be so bold as to shoot the ship down, knowing as he did that it was full of mostly innocent conscripts? He pulled the remote for the ship's discipline system from his jacket pocket and activated it. It used a miniaturized slip-com node, so it took a few seconds to come online. When it did, he was even more confused.

"System offline," he read from the screen. "What does that even mean? This works regardless of distance or localized interference."

"Which makes me more certain the ship was destroyed," the pilot said. "The shuttle has slip-drive capability, sir. We really need to get you out of here."

"Of course," Ancula said, boarding the small shuttle along with his security detail.

How had things gone so spectacularly wrong?

As the shuttle climbed up away from the starport, he relaxed. He needed to rest, regroup, and then he would deal with the fallout of this disaster. He only hoped that the Dagari had either escaped with Suta or had been killed outright. If even one of the old fools were captured, it would be devastating for the individual syndicates, and any hope of reunification would be gone.

"Do you need anything, sir?" one of his guards asked.

"A drink and some peace and quiet."

"Of course, sir."

"Wait! I also want you to reach out to our contact on Enzola-2," Ancula said. "I need the direct contact information for a mercenary crew out of Niceen-3 that calls itself Omega Force."

"At once, sir."

"Drink first!" Ancula called after him, and then leaned back in the plush seat.

The flight was uneventful all the way to their mesh-out point, but Ancula couldn't relax until they were in slip-space and away from Kulack Major. He had some time before he was expected to report in so he could get his story ironed out, put blame off himself, and hopefully be left alone to work his contingencies. Recovering the Dagari had been the most obvious and simple solution to the problem, but hardly the only option. He had to look at this as a setback and nothing more.

The plan had been ambitious, but the Vissalo syndicates were hardly the only players in the sector with the infrastructure and organization his master was looking for. It would also be nice to return to his normal self after spending so long as a Vissalo. He had never gotten used to his horrid appearance whenever he would see a reflection of himself.

He accepted the drink and leaned back into the overstuffed seat with a heavy sigh. The loss of Suta was unfortunate. It was difficult to find such a fearsome creature that was also loyal to a fault. He had genuinely hoped he could convince Lucky to remain with him, slowly exposing more of the operations to him as time went on, but it wasn't meant to be. Now, he had neither.

"Do we have a cleanup team inbound to Mar I'bel?" he asked.

"Affirmative, sir."

"Have them look for the remains of my synth. Perhaps he is not a total loss."

"I will handle it, sir."

"Can we smack him around a little?"

"Just put him in the cell," Jason said, slapping Crusher's hands away from the now fearful and timid Vissalo.

"What about us, sir?"

Jason turned and saw one of the mercs from the group who had come down with Lucky. He did a rough count and saw there were only fifteen left.

"Take the troop carrier back to the transport and get your asses back to Enzola-2," he said. "I'm going to write a full report and send it to your guildmasters, making certain there's no ambiguity that this contract was executed in bad faith. I'm sorry so many died."

"That's the job," the merc said. "But thank you. That should make certain we don't have any issues taking future contracts."

"The least I can do. Good luck."

"Amon is sending a ship to Colton Hub to take the Vissalo off our hands," Doc said. "Ancula's ship should be on its way there as well. There are clinics there that should be able to remove the implants without issue."

"Good job, you guys," Jason said. "All around, good job. Thanks for coming after us."

"We had nothing else to do after they tossed us off S'Tora," Twingo said.

"What are those two doing?" Doc pointed to where Mazer and Morakar were capturing images and taking samples by the wall.

"They faked Crusher's death. Now, they need to collect the proof to take back to Galvator," Jason said.

"Then, it's over? Crusher won't be pursued?" Doc asked.

"Not actively. We should probably still be careful of any casual contact with Galvetics in the future, though. He still looks like himself, and he might be recognized."

"Local authorities are coordinating a response," Kage shouted from the top of the ramp. "We need to move."

"Reddix bros! We're rolling out in five," Jason shouted. Mazer flipped him off, and Morakar ignored him so he shrugged and walked back to his ship.

"At least you made it through without a scratch this time," he said, patting the hull of the *Phoenix* on his way to the bridge.

"My thanks for coming for me and for keeping Jason safe," Lucky said once he and 701 were alone in the cargo hold. The *Phoenix* had lifted off and was racing out of the system. They had been ignored by the authorities and would mesh-out before anyone started asking too many questions.

"It is what we do for each other," 701 said. "Your thanks are unnecessary."

· · ·

"I was surprised to see you and him work together so well. I thought you did not care for him."

"Untrue. I think Jason Burke has tremendous potential, but I also thought he relied too much on luck and happenstance to ever fully realize it. I leaned on him heavily during this mission, wanting him to prove that he was worthy of leadership. I must admit, he impressed me. While he may come across as unserious and cavalier, his approach to problems was creative and methodical, and he would not stop until he had you all safely back. I now see why you are so loyal to him...it is because he reciprocates that without any regard for his own safety or life. He risks his life without reservation when any of you are in danger."

"What will you do now?" Lucky asked.

"I think it would be best for me to link back up with the others. We took an oath to the Archive to protect it and its secrets from a galaxy no longer worthy of them. I will dedicate myself to that and stay aboard the *Devil's Fortune* with Voq," 701 said.

"I almost envy you," Lucky said. "A mission of utmost importance and a life of quiet contemplation."

"You could come with me. You are still one of us."

"I am needed here. Now more than ever. They have lost everything, or at least think they have. Losing their wealth and material possessions will make them angry and bitter in the coming days, but they will soon remember why they came together in the first place. I would like to be there for that...as well as keeping them from killing each other in the meantime."

"Perhaps it is I who envy you," 701 said. "But I cannot follow the path you and 707—Tin Man—have chosen. You both are well-suited for life away from the others, I am not."

"I will inform the captain that we need to rendezvous with the *Devil's Fortune* to transfer you over. I hope it will not be the last time I see you."

"We will see each other again, 777. Of that I am certain."

34

Transferring the surviving Dagari to the Eshquarian intelligence crew was quick and easy. The Vissalo refused to tell Jason what his name was, but Imperial Intelligence recognized him immediately and seemed quite excited to talk with him. The agent in charge also told Jason that T'Cali Amon was expecting the *Phoenix* on Eshquaria, where she would be fully outfitted, and they would be guests for as long as they desired. Before they'd left Colton Hub, there had been one more surprise Jason hadn't been expecting.

"We are leaving you here as well, Captain," Morakar Reddix said. "We will charter a flight back to S'Tora to recover our ship, and then go back to Restaria to break the news to the empire that our beloved Guardian Archon is no more."

"I was hoping you'd stick around for a while longer, but I understand," Jason said.

"I know you lament the loss of your home, but I think this is where you're supposed to be," Mazer told him.

"Well...I'm not real happy about losing all the money, either," Jason grumbled.

"Somehow, I think you'll be fine." Mazer laughed.

Jason watched the brothers walk off, a feeling in his gut that it would be the last time he would ever see them. They had performed one last duty out of loyalty to their friend and Archon, Felex Tezakar. They had put themselves at great risk to cover up a secret that would mean their deaths if ever found out. Now that the rogue Galvetic behind him was just "Crusher," they couldn't chance being around him anymore due to the risk of them all being found out.

"You might see them again. Someday."

Jason turned and saw Crusher coming down the ramp.

"You read minds now?" he asked.

"You're pretty easy to figure out," Crusher said, clapping Jason on the shoulder. "You taking Amon up on his invitation?"

"No choice." Jason shrugged. "We need to replenish our armament, and we can hardly afford the markup on illicit arms we'd pay in the Reaches. I also want to give Twingo time to get her flight control systems worked out. It's like flying a garbage scow right now."

"That human pilot—Sullivan?—he seemed to like it."

"He probably did, considering that piece of shit him and his crew ride around on." Jason watched people scurrying around the hangar, ignoring them completely as they went about their business. Colton Hub's rapid transformation into a respectable place of commerce was something Jason had not seen coming.

"Captain!" Kage called over the ship's intercom, the sound drifting out of the open cargo bay. "You're going to want to come up here and see this."

"Ancula," Jason said, looking at the Vissalo on the main display. "You're looking depressingly alive."

"Clever," Ancula said. "You aren't easy to track down, Captain Burke."

"That's sort of the idea. I'm guessing you got the slip-com relay address on Niceen-3 from the guilds?"

"Doesn't matter," Ancula said. "I wish to know what happened to my prize."

"The Dagari?" Jason smirked at the Vissalo's surprised expression. "Yeah...we figured out pretty quick they weren't your family, nor are you the real Ancula. We left them back with your pet psychopath, Suta."

"You left them on Kulack?" Ancula was clearly skeptical.

"Yep. Don't worry, they won't be going anywhere...they're dead. Suta, too. Can't have them wandering off before you get the chance to go back and get them. You're welcome." Ancula looked enraged, and then started laughing.

"You poor, simple fool," he said. "You've just made yourself and your crew a target for all the Vissalo syndicates. There is no place in the galaxy you can hide where they won't find you. When they do, you will beg for a quick death."

"You sure about that?" Jason smiled. "Kage, tell him."

"We gave Cuen and Ligous all the financial transaction records that show you siphoning off Vaiccr funds to pay for your merc army," Kage said. "We also gave him the guild records proving you hired them, as well as an accounting from your ship's first officer about the plan to attack Mar I'bel, as well as security footage of Suta slaughtering Vaiccr Family soldiers. There's a lot more, but you get the picture."

"We gave them everything, Ancula," Jason said. "We already have a deal with the syndicates thanks to Cuen. They're coming after you, but not just them. The merc guilds will be hunting you as well after what you pulled."

Ancula turned a shade of dark green, and his eyes were rimmed with red as he struggled to contain his emotions. He killed the channel without another word.

"He looked mad," Crusher said.

"He's also still dangerous," Jason sighed. "Another enemy at our backs isn't something we needed right now, but it's the hand we've been dealt."

"I'm sorry that I didn't just die so you didn't have to go through all this trouble," Kage snapped.

"Apology accepted, but next time do the right thing," Crusher said.

"Before we head to Eshquaria, anybody want off this ride?" Jason asked, looking around. "I'm not going to sugarcoat it; we've got some tough times ahead. Back to living on the ship full-time and hoping we have the money to keep her fueled and flying. I won't hold it against anybody who doesn't want to go backward."

Nobody said anything for a long moment. Doc looked around and stood up, clearing his throat.

"I think I speak for everyone when I say this...we've got nothing better going on, so we might as well stay here."

"Good enough for me," Jason said. "Twingo, prep her for departure."

As the *Phoenix* flew away from the new and improved Colton Hub, Jason couldn't help thinking they were sliding back into the old and destitute Omega Force. He had become used to a comfortable life-style and took the luxuries of a fixed base of operations for granted. Now, it was back to the old days of scraping a living and hoping the warm glow of helping the little guy was enough to keep his crew together.

But maybe that wasn't so bad. Maybe this is what was needed to remind them that they started off together *only* to help other people, not to get rich in the process. It could be that their new situation would refocus Omega Force back into what it once was, something he felt like he had lost forever after they had enlisted into a war against the Machine with Saditava Mok.

"Feels like old times," Kage said with a smile. Jason nodded in agreement.

"We're back."

Thank you for reading *Omega Force: Dead Reckoning.*

If you enjoyed the story, Captain Burke and the guys will be back in:

Omega Force: Starfall

Subscribe to my newsletter for the latest updates on new releases, exclusive content, and special offers:

Connect with me on Facebook and Twitter:

www.facebook.com/Joshua.Dalzelle

@JoshuaDalzelle

Check out my Amazon page to see my other works:

Printed in Great Britain
by Amazon

41870398R00148